The Interview

A Novel

By

Christopher McDonald

<u>Other Books</u>
Serum

<u>Social Media</u>
facebook.com/author.christophermcdonald
Twitter: @ChristopherPMCD
Intagram: ChristopherPMcDonald

This book is for everyone in my life that told me I could be whatever I wanted to be. I wanted to be a storyteller.
So here we begin...

Chapter 1

What Happened

"Now... tell me what happened today January 16," a soothing woman's voice said, in the recorder, from the opposite side of the large mahogany table.

"You're a doctor, you tell me," was the reply. After a long sigh, Dr. Williams took off the black Prada reading glasses and sat back in the black leather interrogation chair. "Well, there is not much I can tell you. The courts asked me if I would be willing to sit and talk with you." The doctor leaned her head to the side as if waiting for a reply from the interviewee; instead of a reply he just looked down at his hands in restraints as they lay on the table.

He said, without taking his eyes off his hands, "What does the judge want from me? Why do they have me here? All the police have to say is,

The Interview

'why did you kill them', but I didn't." He then took his eyes off of his hands; his breathing quickened, and then he looked at her in a state of distress. Quickly after their eyes met, for a brief moment, he returned to staring at his hands again and slowing his breathing to normal. Dr. Williams stayed silent during this exchange trying to not interrupt and to let him get out whatever it was on his mind. As he stared at his hands he mumbled, "I didn't do it... I didn't do it."

"What didn't you do George? I'm not judging" She said in her most empathizing voice. Deep down inside as she looked over the file waiting for a response, she was saying to herself 'you bastard how could you.' Never before in her many years as a clinical psychologist had she ever seen such a horror.

"But I didn't do it!" he yelled as he slammed his cuffed hands on the table. This startled her enough to stimulate the flow of adrenalin, and cause her to look up."

"What didn't you do, George?" trying to determine what caused that little episode; she fixed her eyes on him again.

"You know." George said.

"No... I don't know. If you tell me what it is they say you did, I can help you," she replied with a concerned look while he stayed fixated on his bound hands. "You stated that they were asking you why you killed them, them who?"

The Interview

"I don't know," was the quick and sharp reply. But he did know. What he did not know is how and why it all happened, seemingly around him, with no ability to alter things. Thoughts of the events of the day ran through his mind as he stared down at his hands in wonder.

There was a long awkward silence where George started to shake his head back and forth like saying NO. His eyes still on his hands; he rocked back and forth in his chair like in a rocking chair.

"George... I will go now and let you think for a while all you have to do is call for me when you need me. Okay?" She pointed to the mirror on the wall and said, "I will be just on the other side." She the stood up from her chair and began to walk to the door; she paused and looked back to see if he was ready to talk. All he did was to continue to rock to-and-fro, eyes fixed on his hands. She sighed with disappointment and walked the next two steps to the door, opened it, and stepped out of the room.

Once out of the room the two lead investigators in the case greeted her. "What is wrong with you both? You have obviously scared this man to-death. Do you know that when people enter this mental state, they may never snap out of it?"

"No, you have it all wrong Lady. This man would not talk from the beginning we did nothing but ask him why he pushed a coworker in-front of that bus." The tall deputy sheriff said in their defense.

The Interview

"Then how did you ask him?" she tilted her head like she didn't believe them, and looked at them in the eyes in disbelief.

"We did nothing wrong to that psycho, damn-it. We have two witnesses who say that he pushed that poor woman in front of the bus. She was only twenty-three, for God's sake." Sam, a tall but overweight investigator, replied back to the harsh comment. For some reason, Sam hated the suspect from the beginning. It probably had something to do with the fact his little sister was best friends with her.

"Well, you two may think you did nothing wrong, but you placed some degree of damage on his psyche. This man is in a very fragile state now. I want him to be kept in that room until I return. Do you both understand…? I have to make a couple of phone calls to the hospital, and I will be back in five? No one is to enter that door until I return. DO I MAKE MYSELF CLEAR?" Dr. Williams didn't know where this commanding role came from but for the moment it worked and she just went with it.

Both responded with, "Yes Doctor."

Dr. Williams nodded and turned to walk away to the nearest empty office to place a call to her assistant. Once inside she took a breath and collected her thoughts.

After a moment to rest she picked up the phone and dialed her assistant John. "John I'm glad I got a hold of you. I need some things from my office, bring me: a blank case file with plenty of paper, I need my digital recorder, and refill for my

Mont Blanc." She loved to use this pen when taking notes. This was the pen her mother gave her when she graduated Harvard University.

"Is there anything else?"

"Yes, bring me a Big Mac and fries with a coke, and apple pie from McDonald's," was her response.

"Are you joking," he asked?

"No, no, not at all. This one is in pretty bad shape. Thanks a lot John, please hurry. I need to get back in there as-soon-as-possible. I will be in the upstairs interrogation room 'A' of the east side precinct." She said her good-byes and hung up the phone.

She then got up and walked out. She went down the hall to the mirror room where the two officers stood. The mirror room was a room on the other side of the interrogation room like the one in all of those movies with interrogators. This room was dark so that anyone in the interrogation room would not be able to see through the one-way mirror.

"Did he say anything while I was gone?" she asked.

Sam said, "No not yet."

They all just stared and watched him rock back and forth. Dr. Williams said, "I need some more background on what happened to his alleged victim. I know that he was seen pushing her out in front of the bus. But who was she, what do know about her? How did he know her?" While asking the investigators she never took her eyes off the one way for a second she watches him the whole time.

Sam started. "All I know about Whitney, that was her name is that she worked in the same building as George. She worked a few cubicles away from George. Her best friend and roommate told us that George had asked her out on numerous occasions, but she had turned him down *nicely* every time. The roommate talked about what a nice person she did not ever want to hurt anyone's feelings. One day George got a 'yes' out of Whitney. After the date, the roommate told us that the Whitney came home mad and didn't want to talk about what happened. The roommate said she just went to bed and figured that they would talk the following night. The next day Whitney got ready to go to work, and according to the roommate seemed fine. She was humming a tune while brushing her hair. The roommate indicated that the mood had seemed to vanish overnight.

The next thing we have is that other co-workers around the building saw her. She told one lady that she thought she 'would be bad today, and go out to eat a hotdog for lunch.' There are a few witnesses that say that he pushed her in front of that bus."

"Sounds like some form of rejection happened to him on the date to make him mad enough to kill her on his lunch break." Never taking her eyes off that mirror Dr. Williams speculated.

The Interview

The other members of the room then turn to look back through the mirror he still sat there rocking and shaking his head NO.

"Why do you think he is doing that rocking thing?" Eddie another officer in the group asked.

Dr. Williams replied "I'm not sure yet. It could be shock, even though this is not typical behavior for someone in shock."

"There is something else." Eddie said while removing his patrol hat. "There were several other incidents that happened that day too. One in particular was when the girl got run over by a bus; George went back to the building where his boss Mr. Sweet met him at his desk. By that time, we were down on the street investigating the death of Whitney. George was asked to come to his bosses office where there were termination papers lying on his desk with his name on them.

Something happened in that office. I don't know what, Mr. Sweet's secretary does not recall hearing any loud talk or anything that resembled a fight. All that I can tell you is that I was down on the street photographing Whitney when... Splat... That was the first time I saw Mr. Sweet, when he hit the ground, that is."

"What did the termination papers imply? Why was he being fired?" She squinted her eyes but never taking them away from the mirror, Dr. Williams asked.

"Well, it wasn't filled in, all it said was: harassment of company employees and taking too long for lunch. Under the comments section in a different handwriting, there was 'I didn't mean too.' We can only speculate that it was George's handwriting. We couldn't get him to admit to this."

"He was reminded of Whitney, and the rejection. What happened next?" asked Dr. Williams?

"Well, this is a funny thing." Eddie replied. "The witnesses on the street said that he ran back to the building, and Sweet's secretary said that he just walked out of the administrative office like nothing had happened, and even told her that Mr. Sweet did not want to be disturbed. He then was reported to have gone back to his desk and collect his things, turning off his computer, and seemed to be going home."

"In the case file I read that he was being implemented on four murders. What else happened?" asked Dr. Williams.

"Sam take this one for me, I have to pee."

"Ok, Eddie will do. Well, he walked out of the building and went past the crime scene where the two corpses of his former associates lay. He was then reported going down the subway steps near the office.

"Wait a minute," Dr. Williams interrupted. This time she took her eyes off the mirror and looked Eddie in the eyes. "You are telling me he just walked right out of that building and no one recognized him from the street." Dr. Williams said shaking her head in amazement.

The Interview

"Yep, he walked right past us and I didn't know him from Adam," was the quick response.

"Ok, continue on." Still shaking her head in amazement she turns to look back at the mirror as to observe the rocking George.

"Once on the subway dock there were several people who recognized George from work. I suppose they were coming back from lunch or something. One reportedly walked over and said something about the date the night before. Other witnesses said that he yelled out 'I don't want to talk about it, GO AWAY.' so he turned to walk away when he was reportedly pushed by George in front of an oncoming train."

"Who was this guy?" Dr. Williams interjected.

Eddie replied back "Well he was reportedly a very good childhood friend of George's. His name was Harry Walsh. He went to College with George and was his senior year roommate. He worked in the same building as George but for a different Company."

"Ok, I'm back I had to go." Eddie said. "Where did you get to?"

"I'm just at the part where George pushed his friend on to the tracks."

"Hold on guys. Haven't you received the footage from the subway security camera yet?" Dr. Williams asked with a puzzled look on her face.

"They should have it for us to review by 9:00 tonight." Sam replied.

The Interview

"So you are going on what witnesses said up to this point?"

"Yes," Sam said.

"Ok then go on," she said with a sigh looking back at the mirror.

Sam started back in. "This is where the witness's stories get a little strange. Some say they heard him yelling for help from the bottom of the tracks. Others say that he just sat there frozen breathing deeply for those few seconds before the train struck. One thing their stories have in common is the fact that all the people on the platform could not move. Frozen in fear, I guess? They all said how much they wanted to help him but just could not move."

Just then a clerk walked into the room and said to Dr. Williams "there was a man downstairs that said you needed him to bring you a few things?"

"Yes it should be John send him up," was the reply. She then turned to the mirror and looked in on George. He had stopped rocking back and forth and had his head on his hands not saying anything.

The next person to enter the room was none other than John carrying a large black briefcase and a McDonald's sack.

"You called him to bring you dinner?" Sam asked with some surprise.

"John this is detectives Sam Ettles and Eddie Browner. Sam, Eddie, this is John, my assistant. And No this isn't for me, it is for George."

The Interview

Sam said in a rude sort of voice. "What you are telling me is if I commit four homicides in one day that I will get catered McDonald's by my state issued shrink."

"This is for him. I need him to trust me. If I go in and give him dinner and let him eat in peace, he should be ready to talk afterward. I will then go in with some coffee and this apple pie." She removed the pie from the bag while talking. "We will then sit down and have a nice conversation."

"I hope to hell this works," said Eddie.

"It will just trust me guys. Now one of you needs to go in there with me and unlock his hands," said the doctor.

"Hell no; I'm not going in there with the man that killed these people, and unlock his handcuffs. You must be crazy lady," Eddie snapped.

"I will assume full responsibility if he does anything out of line. Now come-on." she demanded.

They both walked through the door that faced George's back, and shut it behind them. George did not turnaround but just sat there.

"George its Dr. Williams again I was wondering if you were hungry. I brought you McDonald's. I hope you like Big Macs?" she said in a calming voice. "Now I'm going to have Officer Eddie here unlock your handcuffs and let you eat. The thought of no cuffs excited him, and he sat up straight.

The Interview

Eddie walked over and took off the handcuffs saying, "It's, detective, doctor." He then stuck the cuffs back to his belt clip.

Dr. Williams walked over and placed the McDonald's bag and the coke down in front of him and said, "Eat up, and we will talk later, ok." He does not move or say a-thing. She turned to walk out of the room.

As she goes through the door, George said, "Thank you."

She replied, "Your welcome. We will talk when you are through." She left the room with the officer and locked the door. They went back to the mirror room to observe him eat.

"Now you just got to the part where he was down on the tracks and everyone wanted to help but couldn't so what now?" She said in a very skeptical voice.

"Let's take a seat for the next part." Sam said. They all sat down at the table so that they could all see the prisoner.

"Now back to the story, of course, you know what happened next, the train hit his friend. George left the subway while everyone was screaming and proceeded to walk home. We were nearby and ran over to see what all of the commotion was about. Eddie ran into the subway tunnel and heard the people screaming."

"Yeah, an old man told me 'the man that pushed him was on his way south. So I ran to catch up with him, using the description they gave me. He was the only one carrying a box full of office supplies on the street. I told him to hold still while I cuffed his hands. I radioed in my position and verified his identity on his driver's license.

I asked him why he did it, and he just said, 'did what.' That was all I asked him because by then there was a patrol car pulling up beside me. The officer helped me place him in the car and give me a ride back to meet my partner, Sam."

Sam jumped in and said. "This is where we had the patrol officer take George down to the station.

We began to secure the third-crime scene and sign reports to send the first two bodies to the morgue. By this time, it was two in the afternoon. We had gotten the person responsible for the three murders.

Then we get a radio call that an officer had been hit on the side of the road next to his patrol car. Apparently the man in the back seat pushed him into traffic. Of course, the dispatcher had sent officers to the scene we could not go but we knew that we were missing our lead suspect. They called for us to go to that scene once we were finished with the subway murder. That is when we got the news that the man in the back seat was wandering down the road in his handcuffs."

Eddie started in, "The witnesses said that when the cop got to the back seat and opened the door that he was flung into oncoming traffic. Along with the door the officer was crushed by a minivan traveling south. George was picked up a fifteen yards from the scene. We transported him to the station with no problems.

"So let me get this straight. He was seen pushing this guy out with his feet?" Dr. Williams asked. "All of this is a little strange. First of all how did the witness in the subway know he was heading south? You said they were all in the tunnel."

Sam replied, "Well yeah he had to push him with his feet, and why is the witnesses story such a big deal. We caught him."

"Well, the prosecutor will certainly ask this. I wonder why the cop had to go and open the door in the first place." Dr. Williams asked. "This cop also went to the door facing traffic. Why would he do this on a busy city street?"

Eddie noted, "Sometimes people will try to fake a heart attack or choking to get a cop to open the door. I think he was trying to get away."

"Well, I assume that the officer was killed, and that was his fourth victim?" Dr. Williams noted.

"Yep, that's it he was dead at the scene." Eddie added.

"Doc I think he's done with the Big Mac now." John stated. "Here is your briefcase."

"Thanks. It's time to go to work." she replied.

"Are you going in there without him in handcuffs?" Sam asked.

"Yes. We will be fine. One last thing what was the officer's name?"

The Interview

Eddie and Sam said in unison "Marcus Booth."

Chapter 2

The Interrogation

"Are you done yet George?" Dr. Williams asked while entering the interrogation room.

"Yes. Thank you again I didn't get a lunch today." He sighed and placed the Big Mac carton into the sack it originated.

"Do you mind if I sit-down and talk for a while?" She advanced toward the opposite side of the table.

"No I don't mind but all you will find out is that it didn't happen the way everyone said." George started to shake his head to the sound of Dr. Williams's footsteps. As she came closer, he could feel his heart beat increase. His composure changed for every step she took toward the table. He became more stiff and nervous.

Dr. Williams got to the table and sat her briefcase on the floor next to the chair. She took a seat and pulled from the case her recorder. She then placed the recorder on the table between them. "They are making coffee now and will bring it into us shortly. The pie I got for you, do you want it now or with the coffee?

"With the coffee is fine with me, thanks."

"Now... George, I must have your permission to record this conversation. Do you give me such rights?" Dr. Williams asked.

"Yes you can record this conversation." George answered.

"Thank you. This is Dr. Angelica Williams and George Paterson on January 16, at 8:17 p.m. Now that unpleasant thing is over with. George we can start now?

"That's fine." George replied.

"Now, at what time did you wake up this morning George? Do you recall?"

"Every morning I wake up at 6:00 a.m." George answered.

Dr. Williams took a yellow legal pad out of her briefcase along with a black Mont Blanc pen. "Now tell me do you wake up by alarm, or do you wake up on your own?" She opened the pen refill package and started to replace it as he began to speak.

"I mostly wake up about one minute before 6:00 and watch my alarm go off. I don't know why I set the alarm. I guess I set the alarm so that if one day I don't wake up on time there will be something there to remind me."

Now that the Mont Blanc has been refilled she writes 'Wakes up at six on his own' on the notepad. "Can you now tell me what you did next, after you got out of bed? Tell me step by step, and walk me through your average day."

"Well Like I do every morning, I get into the shower and wash my hair. I'm in there for about fifteen minutes. After I get out I shave and get dressed. I then go to the kitchen and have a big bowl of oatmeal. I read the paper next. Then I start to the subway about 7:15 every morning. I arrived at work at 7:55. I sit at my desk booting up the computer waiting for the time to clock in."

All through this reconstruction of George's day Dr. Williams is taking down notes. She writes out times and order.

"I do all of my daily tasks until 12:00. I go to lunch for one hour and return promptly to clock in. Then I go about my daily tasks."

"Before you go any further; could you go into a little more detail on what your daily task consist of? Please." Dr. Williams flipped her legal pad to a new page.

"Yes. When I get there, I answer e-mails on the code issues I corrected the day before." He answered back.

"I take it that you are a computer programmer." Dr. Williams interrupted.

"No. I mean, I can program, but that is not my job. What I do is look at the program that someone else made for some insurance agency, or bank, and I check it out for errors."

"Is it a good job? Now I want you to be completely honest George."

"Yes I like it very much."

The Interview

"Ok, go on." She writes about his control issue and comfort zone in interrogation.

"Well, I check different programs every day, and sometimes one program runs into a second day. When that happens, I just finish it up the day after and e-mail it back to the programming department and move to the next one." George seemed to feel more comfortable talking now maybe he just was relieved to talk to someone who seemed to care.

Just then the door opened behind George, and all of his security he was feeling drained out of him. He crouched over in a hunched back position like before and returned his stare to his hands.

George knew who had entered the room before anyone spoke. Perhaps he knew because he saw the reflection in Dr. Williams's eyes, he just knew. Just as soon as he knew a flashback of the event earlier crossed his mind. The memory of being beaten into a police car by Sam stood out in his mind as if it were happening all over again. George never looked up from his hands.

Sure enough, Sam's feet were the ones that stepped through the threshold. He walked to the table and said, "Here is the coffee, Dr. Williams. I brought two cups, a carafe, and some creamer if anyone wants some."

Sam turned and looked at George and said, "What the hell's wrong with you."

Dr. Williams quickly responded to this abrupt comment. "That will be all, Sam. Thank you."

"Yes Mam call if you need anything." Sam replied taking his focus off of George. He then turned and walked out.

The Interview

Dr. Williams took down notation of the strange behavior that George exhibited when Sam entered the room.

"Are you ok, George? He is gone now, and I have an apple pie and some coffee for you." George looked up with dilated pupils.

"How do you take your coffee?" Dr. Williams asked while talking, taking the apple pie out of her soft briefcase.

"Black," he said.

"Me too George, I like mine black too." She poured both cups full and pushed one George's way. Also, she pushed the apple pie. George tore into that apple pie like a raccoon in a trash heap. He looked from side to side like an animal looking for predators.

"Ok, now back to the daily routine. You know what George when you're done telling me about your day; I think we can call it a night and finish up tomorrow." She said with some enthusiasm in her voice. By this time, George was almost done with his pie. After scarfing down the pie, he guzzled down the hot coffee behind it.

Gasping for air and setting down his empty cup, he agreed to the terms. He agreed although he had no idea that he would not get to go home and sleep.

"Ok, after you are done for the day what do you do?"

"I clock-out precisely at 5:00pm and head out the building for home. I reenter the subway and spend my 30 minutes on the subway reading a book of some sort. After I get home, I watch the news on the TV in my kitchen while I cook dinner. I have to find out what that damn president has been up to all day. I can't wait until November when we can elect someone new."

Dr. Williams took down the resentment to the president. "Ok, Go on."

"Well, after I eat, and cleanup; I go read more on my books. At 9:00 every night I go to bed. Well, every night except for this one."

"I guess, so it is 9:15 now. Ok, George I have a few more questions before we hit the hay. "What kind of books do you read on the train and at home after dinner?"

"I read all sorts of thing, like horror, love stories, medical journals, and all sorts of other interesting stuff."

She took down notation of the types of books and said, "One more question George. Do you have any phone conversations with anyone while at home? Do you talk to your mom or dad?"

"No, they are both dead. I really have no one to talk to." He said this like a sad person and began to look at his hands again as if he were ashamed.

"Ok, George I think this about wraps it up for tonight we will continue tomorrow. Now don't be frightened Eddie or Sam will come in here to take you to your cell." George's heart sunk when he heard the word cell. He came to the realization that he was not going home tonight and resumed the posture from before.

"Goodnight George." Dr. Williams stood up and packed her things to get ready to leave. "George. Why so sad?"

The Interview

George took his eyes off his hands for a moment and said, "I was hoping to go home." Just like before he put his concentration back on his hands.

"Well, tonight will not be a night for that. There are a few things we must clear up first. We still have a lot to talk about, and I will be back tomorrow to discuss them with you." Dr. Williams snapped her leather briefcase back together. "Now cheer up. I can assure you nothing bad will happen to you tonight ok."

George nodded as if saying yes. Dr. Williams stood and walked to the door. "Night." Then she was gone through the door from which she had entered a little more than an hour before.

Chapter 3

The Cell

When the door shut from Dr. Williams leaving, Sam opened the door and stepped in. George could feel his presence. He walked slowly to the back of the chair that George sat at. Sam placed his hands on George's shoulders. George did not turnaround; he could feel Sam's beer belly press against the back of the chair and through the slats.

Sam said, "Put your hands behind your back, murderer!" with this demand he pushed George forward onto the table. When George's face hit the tabletop, his nose made a cracking noise. As George cried out in agony blood ran down his face and onto his orange inmate scrubs. Sam just said, "Shut up you Killer." George continued to moan and groan while Sam fastened handcuffs on him.

Sam pushed Him out of the chair and onto the floor of the interrogation room. There he lay on the

The Interview

hard cold floor, pain shooting through his nose; wishing he could do something, anything that would get him out of this situation. But, of course, this was impossible. He was helpless. He wondered why this was happening. He had no memory of hurting anyone.

The next thing George knew he was being picked up by the collar of his uniform, and being shoved toward the door. Sam opened the door for George, and waiting outside was Eddie. Both officers grabbed George by one wrist or the other to escort him to his holding cell.

As they walked Sam reviled to George why this killing spree was getting under his skin.

"Why did you do it?" Sam asked. "What could have been your possible motive? These were all good people."

"Why did I do what?" George questioned.

"Don't play that with me you little shit-head." Sam said with force. "What did Whitney do to you that drove you to all of this?"

"I didn't do anything to her, I swear." This was the most sincere answer he gave all night. Blood still ran down his face.

"Did you even know her for who she was or did you just date her once and throw her out?" Sam asked as they turned right at the end of the hall. "She was my sister's best friend. You little prick." Sam punched George in the mouth and caused his lip to bleed in-sync with his nose.

Eddie yelled, "That's enough Sam you will be in a hell-of-a-lot-of trouble when the Sergeant finds out you've been beating the inmates. Besides there is nothing, you can do for her now."

The Interview

They all stand in the hall. "What do you think it feels like to call your best friend, at work, to tell him that you are investigating his sister's homicide? Could you hold your composure then? Hell-no!" Sam roared.

"There is nothing you can do about it now. Beating up on her killer is not going to bring her back. It could cost us our case." Eddie negotiated. We will walk George here to his cell, and not talk the whole way. OK?"

"That's fine," Sam sullenly replied.

George was glad that Eddie was taking up for him; he could now see why the frustration was mounting between Sam and him. George still did not feel that he had done anything wrong. He knew that Dr. Williams would understand and protect him. He had at that moment made up his mind. He would tell her exactly what had happened.

"Turn right here George." Eddie ordered. "Open cell 'C.'"

George was let go by Eddie at the door, and Sam removed the cuffs and shoved him in. The large door clanked shut behind him.

"Let's go Sam," Eddie demanded while Sam looked in disgust at the person he believed to be a killer. Sam finally turned away to leave. George was alone at last.

This being the first time in a jail cell; George paused to take a look around. What he saw was horrifying by his standards. There was a small cot bolted to the floor. On top of the cot was a mattress rolled up with a snap to hold it together. Besides the mattress was a couple sheets; he leaned over to feel them. Of course, he was to sleep on less than a hundred-thread count, and on something, (he didn't quite know what it was,) but it wasn't cotton, it felt like sand paper. He then glanced over at the opposite wall to find a toilet-sink combination. There was nothing but grey walls and black floors. The air must have had 95% humidity, and felt cool like 60°

He felt so bad, but not scared. George learned from early on not to be scared of anything; it just lands you in more trouble. He wiped his bloody nose with the orange cover-all and walked the two steps from the door to the rolled mattress. He began to unroll it to make a place to lie. While trying to make the god awful sheets conform to the lumpy mattress, he began to think. 'What do they think they can prove?'

Just as he had everything settled he began to get into bed. The pillow in this case was made into the mattress. He noticed that the bed had no springs and that he was not going to get the best night's sleep.

"Lights out!" yelled a man from down the hall. Five seconds later the lights went out with a loud clank.

George wondered why the hell he yelled that out. As far as he could see when he walked down the hall; he was the only one here. He said to himself, 'Well if they didn't warn me that the lights were going out, and I fell and hit my head or something. Then I could sue them. I could sue them and get money but while you are in here, there will be no way to spend it. I will ask my lawyer about it when he gets here tomorrow.'

The Interview

George's attention was taken away from the lights out situation when he noticed a slight drip in something. Drip... Drip... DRIP... It was driving him crazy he hopped out of bed and walked around his cell trying to find what was dripping. He started at the most obvious place, his sink-toilet. The sink-toilet was not the thing dripping, but he still heard it. He walked over next to the cold bars at the foot of the cot. There he heard the Drip... Drip... coming from the next cell over.

George whispered in his lowest voice. "Hey is there anyone over there? Hey, could you stop that dripping?" By this time, George was sitting on the floor holding on to the bars trying to project his voice out of the cell.

Down the hall, the way George came in sat the night watch officer at his desk. He heard a whisper and started out to find what it was.

"Is there anyone over there? Can you hear me?" WACK... was the sound the nightstick from the night watchman as he slung it to strike George on the nose. George saw him coming and pushed his face back in time. His hands however got whacked by the nightstick.

George jerked his hand back in pain. Screaming at the top of his lungs, "I just wanted to stop the dripping noise. I just want it to stop. It makes my head hurt."

"The night watchman placed his stick back into his holster. "You know the rules, no talking. There is no one over their anyway." George could barely understand him for the pain. "I better not hear another peep out of you tonight. GOT IT?"

"Ok... ok... I'm sorry... I'm sorry..." George said with fear in his voice.

"Get back in bed, and don't talk." The night watchman replied. George obeyed the night watchman orders and went to bed.

The night watchman watched him crawl back into bed moaning in pain. "You better stop that groaning, or I will make life real difficult." George at this time bit his tongue.

As he got into bed, his nose began to bleed again. George could not believe that he was bleeding again; the night watchman did not hit his nose. To top it off, he was getting a real headache. George just wished that this would all go away.

The watchman started to walk away. He paused to say, "Don't let me hear another peep out of you. I'm trying to read a book over-here." The then proceeded to the desk at the end of the hall. He sat down and picked up his book and began to read again.

George sat there in thankful that he went away. He let out the breath he had been holding the last few seconds. He was in unbearable pain. George decided to look at the ceiling and count dots until he went asleep.

DRIP... DRIP... DRIP...

There was that sound again. He stopped counting and squinted his eyes shut wrinkling his brow. The incessant noise made him want to scream. Realizing the consequences of this action, he decided not to.

George began to take his mind off of the dripping. He turned to his side and looked at the wall. He started reading the graffiti on the wall. It was etched stone not written on like you see in high school bathrooms. This was carved in the stone wall. One thing caught his eye. There on the wall was a man being hung. The rope descended from no-where, and at the end of the rope was a man dangling lifelessly with a piece of paper in his hand.

Drip... Drip... The noise was slowly fading in the background as his attention focused on the artwork. He wondered what had gone through this persons mind. 'Why did this person carve this? A warning to show what was to come?'

Christopher McDonald

"Why did that man hit me?" George was whispering to himself. "All I wanted to do is to see if someone was in the next cell to shut that water off." Just then he recognized what he was trying to forget.

DRIP... DRIP... DRIP...

There he lay in the jail cot wondering what he could do to get out of this whole mess. George wondered if telling the truth would get him out of this. 'Would Dr. Williams believe it if I told her? No... I don't think that she will. If she doesn't; there is only one option left... If I have to... I will..." Then he turned and began to look at the man in the carving holding that piece of paper. He wondered what it was. A suicide note or death warrant; like in the medieval times. Slowly thinking about this he

slowly drifted off to sleep letting his worries fade

away.

Chapter 4

Morning

On and off all night George tossed and turned. He had not had more than two hours of sleep when the lights snapped on. The loud noise woke him.

On the other side of town, Dr. Williams woke, to the sound of her alarm; the clock read 5:00am. She hit the snooze twice and finely at 5:10am she crawled out of bed leaving her stockbroker husband to sleep. She went to their bathroom and took a nice warm shower. She went over and over what she could say to George to get him to give the most detail possible. She hoped that she could get him to hone in on each crime as it happened.

The Interview

"Come on scum-bag time to get a shower." A man in uniform shouted. "Get your lazy ass out of bed, scum-bag."

George immediately responded wishing not to have the same thing happen that happened the night before. He did just as the guard demanded; he followed him. The guard took him down the opposite end from which he had arrived. He passed the neighboring cell where he saw the sink with a leaking faucet.

They approached the room at the end of the hall where they told him to strip. George hesitated. It wasn't that he was shy, but he didn't know exactly what was about to happen.

"Now don't be a girly man. Get them damn clothes off, or we will rip them off of you." was the guard's response to George's hesitation.

He did just as the guard asked and removed all of his clothes. The guard then pushed him into a three foot by three-foot room with nothing but a bar of soap on the floor. The door slammed behind him. He was alone again.

George stood there for several minutes on that cold hard tile floor wondering if he would get a real shower. Suddenly there was a loud whaling noise; a loud roar that startled George. The pipes were vibrating above his head as the noise got louder. He was reminded of a story he read where the Nazi soldiers lead a mass of people into the shower and poison came from the pipes. The ice-cold water broke his thought. There he stood for two solid minutes in cold water wishing he were dead.

The Interview

The water eventually warmed up to room temperature. His wounds on his lips, nose, and hands were throbbing as the lukewarm water ran across his face.

A steady stream of water soon came to a halt. He stood there with no towel. The door did not open for five minutes. After a long silence, the guard that shoved him in there finely opened the door. He had fresh clothes for him. He put them on as ordered.

"Follow me dip-wad," Ordered the guard. He slapped handcuffs on George and began to walk past the long wall of jail cells. He walked past the night watchman's desk and back to the interrogation room. On the long walk to the interrogation room, he could not help but think about the guard's comment, 'Dip-wad.' He wondered what the hell a Dip-wad was. What does one do with a wad of dip?

The guard opened the door. "Sit in that chair and don't move. Your lawyer will be here in a few minutes." He removed Georges handcuffs and placed them in his belt.

"I don't want a lawyer." George answered. "All of this will be cleared up today."

"Look man..." The guard looked at him with this look of amazement. "I don't have any power over the lawyer. The judge in this case ordered him to come." George didn't look satisfied. "Look when he gets here; you can be a dumb shit and fire him. Only if you want to," He then shut the door.

7:00am George's hair was still wet as the door opened to the room. In walked a man in a three-piece buttoned-down suit. The man had grey hair. He sat down in front of George and said, "Good morning," he opened a large black briefcase.

George smiled but hid it with his hands. He smiled because the man remained him of the monopoly man. George loved that game.

"I think we should start by going over a plea before your shrink gets here." The monopoly man started shuffling his papers around.

"You're fired." George said.

Monopoly man sat down the papers and said, "Do what son?"

"You're fired. I will clear this entire mess up with my shrink today." George replied "Son do you know what it is you are looking at here. Life in prison or maybe even death," said he monopoly man.

George thought for a moment. He thought about life in prison. He could not take that. Another night like last night Hell NO! George nodded and said, "I want to speak with Dr. Williams first, but you can stay."

"Ok... If you think, you can clear this up with her, you can. But the judge appointed me in this case. I will stay and watch from on the other side of that mirror over there. If you feel, you need me just call for me. I am Mr. Carr."

George smiled and shook his head while Mr. Carr put away his things. "I don't think that I'll need you today thanks," he responded. Mr. Carr got up, walked to the door, and knocked.

"Let me out." The grumpy old man ordered. The door swung open with a bang. This sound startled George and caused him to stare at his hands.

Mr. Carr walked out and shut the door behind him with a clank. He looked at Sam and said, "What the hell is wrong with that boy?"

"I think he's just crazy." Sam answered. "Sane people don't just go around killing people."

Mr. Carr said, "I may have to use that."

At 5:30am Dr. Williams got out of the shower, and began to dress for the day. While she got dressed, she thought what did all of these people have to do with George? Why did he kill them?

After getting dressed, she sprayed some perfume on her chest and started toward the kitchen. She left her husband in the bedroom sleeping. She grabbed an apple, banana, and two cups of yogurt (the kind with fruit on the bottom) as she walked through the kitchen. After stuffing all of this in her purse, she grabbed two spoons out of the drawer and headed to the foyer.

She grabbed her raincoat out of the closet and wrestled it on. She then went over and grabbed her cell-phone, and briefcase, then headed to the door all the while thinking of the complexity of this man's mind.

After she had entered the parking garage, she piled all of her possessions in the back of her black Mercedes-Benz sport-utility. She got in and headed for the ground floor of her buildings parking garage, and out to the street.

One thing she noticed while she drove down the street to the station is that the fog was unusually thick this morning. There was more fog than she had ever seen before. This caused her to drive extremely slowly.

At 6:45am she arrived at the station, and watched from the observation room while the lawyer went in and talked to George. She took out her legal pad and made note of this. Once the lawyer entered the observation room Dr. Williams asked, "Why did he laugh at you?"

"I don't know," answered Mr. Carr sharply. "I guess he thought I was funny. All he wants to do is talk to you." he sighed and took off his bifocals to wipe them with his tie. "I get up extra early to be treated like shit by a court-appointed client. They don't pay me enough." he placed his glasses back on his face and looked at Dr. Williams.

"Well, I will let him sit there for a few moments and see what he does in this isolated condition." Dr. Williams decided out-loud. For the next five minutes, he sat there staring at his hands. He made no move but to blink. "Ok. I think that is enough."

Dr. Williams got up from her chair and walked to the door. "Don't let them interrupt me once I get started." She remembered yesterday when Sam entered the room George's whole affect changed.

"Ok." Mr. Carr said as she walked out the door.

At 7:10am Dr. Williams barged through the door guarded by Officer Sam. "Good morning George," she said as she entered. She walked past him and sat down in her nice comfortable chair. "I will be recording this conversation too."

"Ok." George answered. Dr. Williams took the recorder out of her bag and placed it on the table.

"I brought you something George," she reached into her purse and pulled out the food she packed before. "Do you like apples or bananas?"

George looked up. You could see the hunger in his eyes. In this jail, you got feed one time every day. "Apples," he said.

She pushed the apple toward him. "I also have yogurt. The kind with fruit on the bottom." she pushed one cup over with a spoon lying on top.

"Thank you," he said. He ate the apple as fast as he could while listening to what Dr. Williams had to say.

"What happened to your hand? And look at your nose and lip!" she pointed to his bruises.

"Oh nothing... I was just a-little clumsy in the shower. That's all," he said while looking at the mirror on the wall. Behind the mirror, Sam grinned knowing what the night officer had told him.

"You must be more careful." Dr. Williams stated. "Finish your yogurt and we will talk more. George nodded in agreement. He sucked the yogurt down in three bites.

Chapter 5

The Day Before Yesterday

"Ok, if you are all finished we will begin." Dr. Williams pressed the button on her tape-recorder.

"Before we begin, Dr. Williams, Why are you so nice to me?" George said this in a very curious tone. Pushing his empty yogurt pack to the side, he folded his hands over one another.

"I am nice to everyone that is nice to me." She replied.

"No, there is more to it. Why do you speak to me so nice? Do you think I'm innocent?" He said while looking at her with puppy-dog eyes.

She thought that he was too smart to fall for that old routine 'yes you are innocent.' She took the next logical approach. "I don't know if you are guilty or not, George. I like to think that everyone is innocent until proven guilty. I am nice to you because you have not given me any reason to be cross with you." Dr. Williams realized that this man's mind was more complicated than she thought. He will want to know more things about her. George will want pick at her brain too.

"Last time you told me about what you did in a day. Could you elaborate a little more? On the titles of books that you have read, that is. Dr. Williams said while noting the date and time on her notepad.

"Yes I just got done with <u>Dolores Claiborne</u> by Stephen King." George was interested at the reaction Dr. Williams give him. There was no reaction, but a notation was made on her bright yellow notepad. "Do you read Stephen King or Anne Rice any doctor?"

She lifted her head up from her notepad and said swiftly, "No. I can't say that I have." she noted questions on the notepad to ask in the future. "Do you have anything on the philosophical side that you read?"

"Oh yeah, lots of stuff like Plato, *Harvard Medical Review*, papers by the Pope, and other stuff." He replied.

"That sounds interesting to read about." She noticed that he was more enthusiastic about the Stephen King novel than the medical journal. She waited for a reply or elaboration, but never got one.

"Ok let's go back two days ago, and look at what you did after getting up. I need to know if you did anything out of routine that you normally do not do." she sat back and waited for the reply.

George looked as if he possessed the information but didn't know how to say it. After a long twenty-second silence, he spoke. "I just got up as usual and did all of the things we discussed yesterday." He looked at her notebook trying to make out what she was jotting down.

"Well, when you were on your way to work did you do anything out of the ordinary?" She was looking at him while he took the time to proses this information. She thought he might be playing back his photographic memory. She then noted the time it took for him to arrive at an answer looking down at her watch.

"No nothing out of the ordinary. I just got on the train and rode all the way to work." He looked again as she wrote something in her notebook.

"Ok, then. Did anything happen while at work that seemed to be out of the ordinary?" She watched as he responded immediately.

"Well... I don't ask a girl out every day on the elevator. If that is what you mean?" He looked at her blue eyes with some pride.

She flipped the sheet over and began to note this irregularity. "Whom did you ask out?" Dr. Williams took her eyes off the notepad to see his face as he responded.

"Only the most beautiful girl on my floor, her name is, Whitney Bell." He stuck out his chest and looked proud at his accomplishment.

"What did you say to Whitney, George?" Dr. Williams asked.

"Well... let's see... I just said 'Hi' she said it back. I then asked, 'Hey how-bought we go after work tonight to get some wings and beer at the bar.'." George looked back at Dr. Williams and said,

The Interview

"Can you believe it? She said, 'Well OK.' She said yes finally!" He looked across the table with such pride.

"So you have asked this girl out before?" Dr. Williams stated.

"Yes I have. She would always say things like oh I have plans or no thanks, but this time she actually said yes. He pushed his back upright.

"Was the arrangement to meet you there or were you to pick her up?" Dr. Williams asked.

"Oh, after we got to the 13th floor we set it up. She would meet me at seven o'clock at the bar." He grinned and said, "But she said yes." He looked down at his hands like in his mind he had just accomplished the impossible again. He looked at Angelica again and smiled, saying in his mind, *'yes... yes...'*

Angelica looked strange at him like she knew the mental anguish he went through. She looked down at her notepad and began to write the psychotic style outburst. Dr. Williams wrote in capital letters, "SHE SAID YES." She wondered what the cause of the outburst was. In her mind, she only saw her perfect life. In some way, she had a biased opinion on how his mind worked, not taking in consideration of his adolescence.

"Dr. Williams." She looked from her pad and stared across the table to George. He looked like a puppy in a pet store window. She shook her head acknowledging him. "What did it feel like when your husband asked you to marry him?"

Angelica frowned and said, "How did you know that I'm married?" She then noticed that he was looking down at her hand, on the table; she

The Interview

was wearing a wedding ring. "Oh..." She felt dumb and thought that next interview she did would be done without her rings. It was instinct for her to get up every morning and put on her Cartier watch that her husband give her on their fifth-wedding anniversary, and her wedding set.

"Did you feel all warm and fuzzy inside?" He asked glancing down at his hands. "I felt this way when she said yes. She said yes, and it felt like everything I had ever hoped for had come true. Do you know what I mean?" George placed his hands out in front of him palm up, looking desperately across the table for understanding.

Angelica looked from her paper and said, "Yes I do know what that feeling is like. I guess I did feel that way the day my husband asked me to marry him." She looked back into his satisfied eyes and resumed questioning him. "What did you do after she said yes?"

George replied, "I went back to my desk and began to plan the night's events." He withdrew his hands and began to look at them as if he were worried again. The feeling of warmth he had before, now it was gone, and he was back to feeling sorry again. It was as if he knew in some way he was responsible for the death of Whitney. He knew in his mind that he did not push her, but something in him drove her to kill herself.

"What type of plans did you make?" Dr. Williams asked. Making more notes on her paper.

"Oh... You know. First-date jitters caused me to question what I would wear or what cologne I would put on. Stuff like that. I even remember asking myself what I would eat once I got there.

The Interview

You know, how it would look?" George thought

back on what he did next, but could remember

nothing else.

"Ok then, if that's all you can remember

then we will go on." Dr. Williams drew a line on her

notepad, and wrote, *Leaving Work.* "Ok. What did

you do at the end of the day there at work?" She

places the tip of the Mont Blanc on the paper ready

for his response.

"Well, there was no exception to the-day-

before-yesterday; I closed my computer and left."

George said while folding his hands over and

straightening his back.

Dr. Williams wrote nothing. "Did you pack

up early?" She said.

"No... Well, maybe five or so minutes early.

You won't tell my boss will you? George placed his

feet flat on the floor and slammed his palms on the table. He did nothing but stare in her eyes as she bent down to write about this surprising response. As Angelica's pen began to move George raised his hands from the table and slammed back down, this time in a fist.

"Dr. Williams!" George demanded her attention. "You will not tell my boss will you?" his hands making a tighter fist than before.

"George, I will not say anything to your boss." Angelica looked in his eyes to try to find some other human emotion than anger. Just as he had turned his temper on, he had turned it off. All of his muscles relaxed to the reassuring sound she made. "I won't tell Mr. Sweet anything. You have my word. He doesn't even know you're here."

The Interview

"Ok then..." George said. "He would fire me for sure of he knew I spoke ill of him, or left my desk early." George went back to the usual posture, folded hands, feet crossed, and eyes are looking down.

"Tell me what you did to get ready for the big night." Dr. Williams asked. She finished writing about the boss incident.

"Well, I got home and began to shower. I got out of the shower, and went to my room to pick out what I was to wear that night. I found a nice sports coat with a t-shirt to go under it, and nice slacks. They were not the things I wore to work every day." George looked at Dr. Williams writing furiously in her notebook. "I brushed my teeth and hair then I left." He waited patiently for her to stop writing and lookup with a new question.

"There was nothing unusual about getting ready?" Dr. Williams asked looking up from her pad. "You got ready and just left? What time did you leave the house?"

"What do you do when you get ready in the morning?" George asked. You do the same thing every morning that you did the day before. Getting ready was the same thing that afternoon, but with nicer clothes." George responded like she had asked a stupid question. He folded his hands and cocked his head up with a superior attitude.

"Ok... Then..." She wrote a few more things on her pad.

"Why do you want to know if there was anything unusual about what I do? There is always something out of the ordinary with everything someone does." George became increasingly irritated about the whole questioning process.

"George, I just want to understand everything to make note in my file so that later down the line I may be able to keep up with what was going on." Angelica explained to George, but she would have done better to explain her situation to a brick wall. "Do you understand? I'm just creating a reference point between my mind and yours."

"Ok." George nodded and just agreed with her in an attempt not to take up any more time. He wasn't satisfied but agreed just the same.

"So then after you left did you go straight to the bar? Angelica drew a line on the paper and wrote *to the bar.*

"Yes I got on the Subway and went to downtown where I walked to the bar." George answered nodding his head.

Angelica wanted to know how much he anticipated the night. She already knew the answer before she asked. "Did you get there early?"

George paused before answering as if he suspected her method. "You think I'm desperate don't you?" He clenched his teeth together.

Dr. Williams sat her pen on the table and decided how to handle this. "No, of course, not George... I just want to create a timeline so that when I go back and look at the material I will better understand when all of this happened." She picked back up her pen and nodded to him in a go-ahead fashion.

The Interview

"Ok, I got there an hour early, but that doesn't mean that I'm desperate." George balled his fist in anger and disbelief.

"Thank you George," Dr. Williams said. "Did you sit there and wait the whole time or did you mingle with other people and have a drink?"

"As a matter of fact there was some attractive girl who came and sat beside me. She and I had a drink. She even asked me to go back to her place." George straightened his back and looked proud. "I told her no I was waiting on the most beautiful girl in the world. I think I pissed her off. She rolled her eyes at me and slid off the bar stool, and threw her glass of whisky in my face. She called me a wanker. I don't know what that means, but I know it's not good."

"George she just thought you called her ugly. Dr. Williams said with sympathy. "But go on."

George looked at her with awe. "Oh... Well, I just ordered a rum and coke, and continued to wait. I guess I waited about an hour before she finally showed; right on time." George looked as if he were floating off into nowhere.

"What happened next, George?" Dr. Williams asked. She wanted him to hurry and get to the actual date before the end of the day.

"Well, I just asked her to sit down, and we began to share a bowl of peanuts," George stated. "Next we got a drink. I had a glass of red wine; she had a Jack Daniels tall. This seemed odd to me because women don't usually like that drink." Dr. Williams bit her tongue to keep from making a remark about his hasty generalization as she liked the occasional Jack and Coke.

"Now what happened?" Dr. Williams inquired folding her hands over one another, and hiding her Mont Blanc.

"Well, we began to talk," He said. George paused and looked down at his shoes with no laces in them. "The conversation was about work. We talked about how we have both worked there for years and not gotten promoted. I asked her about her education and how she came to be so smart." George began to ramble as if he remembered something painful. "I asked her several things. But she seemed incredibly angry about the 'So Smart' comment. I told her that I didn't mean it the way it sounded."

Dr. Williams interjected, "This sounded like you were trying to compliment her." She reached her hand out.

"No, you don't understand. I don't know how to talk to women." George put his head on his hands and began to breath heavy.

"George we are going to break away from the subject for a moment. I want you to tell me about your relationship with your parents." Angelica went into psychological mode. "How do you remember the way your father treated your mother?" She wanted to find out how this man had been raised to treat women.

"Well, as far as I can remember my dad treated my mother awful. He was a drunk with many girlfriends. My mother one day came home to him shit-faced drunk and saw him in bed with one of his whores." George grabs the end of the table and squeezes it hard.

"Good George you are doing fine just keep going. I need you to focus and vocalize your anger." Dr. Williams noticed him trying to hide his face.

"I can't," George broke into sobs. He began to sob like a child whose dog just got run over while he sat and watched.

"Yes you can, George." Angelica began to sound more nurturing and caring. "What happened when she saw him? Where were you at the time?"

"I was in the living room. My mom came from the front door and walked down the hall to her room. All I heard was her scream. My father called her a bitch and knocked her down. The woman he was in there with came out." George grabbed harder to the table. He was reliving the whole thing again in his mind.

At this exact moment, the moment in which he was reliving this horror every light in the precinct seemed to go dim. George did not seem to notice. Dr. Williams looked up. Everyone behind the mirror looked at one another. It dimmed so much you could see the outline of every other person in the other room.

George picked his fist up off the table he balled it into a tight fist. "You know I was only eight years old. He didn't think of me."

"You're ok, George," Angelica said calmly.

"He didn't care. My Father was a user and abuser and gave nothing but grief to my mother."

"George I think we need to take a coffee break. I will be right back." Angelica wiped off her glasses and put her pen on the table. She then walked over to the door. "Cream and sugar George?"

"No Black thanks." George said with a surprisingly normal response. Dr. Williams turned, and opened the door then walked out. As she walked out of the room, she remembered, he had black coffee with his apple pie yesterday.

Once out in the hall she began to think about the events in that room and tried to rationalize what she felt. The door next to the one she was leaning against opened. Eddie stepped out and walked over to the visibly shaken doctor.

"Are you ok?" Eddie asked. "You look like he just ran over you with a train." Eddie placed his hand on Dr. Williams' shoulder.

"Yeah, I just had an overwhelming powerful of emotion come over me. I don't know what happened in there, but that is not normally what happens to me. It was like I could feel what he was feeling."

"Well, go get some coffee and we will be in here watching him." Eddie assured her.

Angelica wiped her glasses one last time and walked over to the break room. She was thinking on the way to the coffee room about the moment of intense emotion. She thought about how she saw a little boy in her mind and the feelings that he had toward his mother. 'Damn that must be awful,' she thought.

Once in the break room she sat down for a minute. She thought even harder about the lights going dim. She turned her head and looked up as Sam entered the room.

"You need to hurry the hell up he has a hearing tomorrow in front of Judge Kimberling. He doesn't like lateness on the part of a psychologist." Sam affirmed in an angry, impatient voice, "We would like to all go home sometime tonight too."

"Don't you tell me you smug son-of-a-bitch. I am the doctor here don't you forget it. The judge can't make a move without me signing off first. You will go home when I am done and not a second sooner. Push me, and I will drag this on for days without sleep." His rude remark had empowered her. She needed to get a coffee and get back to work. She now had her mind in order and was ready to go. She lifted her hand up and pointed to the door, "Now get back into the room and watch him until I get back."

Sam put his hands up in the air as he surrendered. Angelica got up from the table and walked over to the counter. She got two-Styrofoam cups and grabbed the carafe with the other hand. She slapped two caps on the cups and headed toward the door.

Dr. Williams walked back into the interrogation room already knowing what she was going to ask him next. She walked over the table where his back was turned to her and sat the coffee next to him. Just then she had an idea. George, are you getting hungry?"

"Just a little," was the calm response.

"Hold on then." She motioned to the one-sided window pointing to the outside. "Eddie," she called while pointing.

She walked out of the door leaving George inside once again. George turned to watch her walk out. Once outside she meets Eddie. "Is my assistant in there?"

"Yeah, he's here." Eddie shook his head.

"Will you ask him to order us a medium pizza with some money from my account, and go ahead and order you guys some?" Angelica thought that he would talk better with something to eat. "Have him get us one of those two-liter cokes." Eddie shook his head yes again. "Thanks you're a dear."

She turned and walked back into the room where George sat. "I just had my assistant order us a pizza. I assume you do like pizza?"

"In this case doctor you would be right in that assumption." George felt his stomach start to growl at the thought of pizza.

"It has been some time since I have eaten pizza. That would be a good lunch."

"May I ask you something Dr. Williams?" George said while placing his hands together on the table in front of him.

"Yes you may," she answered.

"Do you think I have the capacity to kill?" George said in a serious tone.

"In my opinion everyone can kill." Dr. Williams said as she sat across from George. She picked up her pen and began to write about the situation of her emotional state.

"Now George, do you think your condescending tone towards Whitney is related to the way you remember your father treating your mother?" Dr. Williams made note of this on her pad. While George answered she poured the coffee from a glass carafe.

"I think it is a possibility. I don't mean the things that I say after I say them. If you know what I mean." George looked in more concerning view from this point on; now that he knew that Dr. Williams' professional opinion was that he could kill.

"After the 'So Smart' comment what happened?" Dr. Williams inquired.

George picked up his cup of coffee and took a sip making one of those anointing slurping noises. "The date got rocky from there on. See I really liked Whitney; that is why I fumbled like I did. I had not been on many dates before. This was my first." George put his cup of coffee back on the table.

"Well, what happened next. I got us a table and placed an order for me. She then ordered a plate of fish. I upset her with what I did next; I asked the waiter if the fish was from a local lake because there is mercury in that lake, and I was concerned." George folded his hands back together now. "I didn't want her to get sick from the fish on our first date. We began to talk more about work when I noticed a girl sitting at the table beside us. I guess through the course of conversation I looked at her a little too much. Whitney noticed and got up

from the table. She said, 'I'm going to the restroom.'
I had waited for thirty minutes before I had
someone go and check on her. I had our food
wrapped up, and I left after an hour of waiting."
George proceeded to drink more coffee.

"That's it?" Angelica sounded disappointed.
"It sounds to me that she just ran from you... Well,
just tell me what you did after this."

George putdown his coffee and said,
"Nothing much. There was nothing else to do by
this time it was late. I decided to talk with her the
next day at work, and I went home. I did my usual
when I got home. I took a shower and went to bed."

After a long silence Eddie entered the room and said, "Pizzas here."

Angelica looked across the table to the door, and said, "Bring it in here I'm starving." Eddie did as she asked and brought one of the two boxes of pizza in the room with a bottle of coke and two cups placed on top the two-leader bottle. He sat it on the table between Dr. Williams and George.

"Thank you Eddie." Angelica nodded her head while she watched Eddie walk out the door. "Ok, now George, tell me what you felt after being dumped; if you don't mind me being blunt." Dr. Williams while waiting on the response opened the pizza box and put it in the middle of the table. She set a slice out on a napkin for her to let cool.

"Well, I felt that I had no right to get mad because I had opened my mouth. See I had never been on a real date, and I was a bit nervous."

George reached his hand in the box to get a slice while talking. "I guess I was a bit angry, but I had no harsh feelings towardWhitney."

She picked up a slice of pizza and brought it close to her mouth. Holding the pizza right outside her lips, she said, "Surely you felt some anger. No normal person can go through what you did and feel no anger." She continued to take a bite of pizza.

"I was angry but there was aggression toward me not her. I was the person that I was angry with." George picked up a slice of pizza

Angelica took a drink of Coke and asked, "What was going through you mind as you left the restraint?"

"I was thinking of the tip. I had left the waitress a big tip. I had placed a one hundred-dollar bill on the table for a fifty-dollar tab and walked out with food in hand. The waitress had a good payday that day."

"You did not go back to get it?" Angelica asked.

"No, I just headed to the subway. I decided to go home by subway because any cab money I had gone to the waitress. I just pulled out my weeklong pass and went through the subway. It was paid for." His voice sounded regretful over his choice of tip funds. He sounded like he was slipping into a state of melancholy.

"Was there anything memorable on the subway?" Dr. Williams asked.

"There was this one woman that had a newspaper in her hand reading it across from me. I looked at the outside to see the article on the front.

The Interview

It was about Martha Stewart and something yet again about insider trading."

"What was so unusual about that?"

"Well, it was not the paper or Martha Stewart it was the woman reading the paper. I looked up to see her fixated on me. She was fixated on my face. The stare she gave me was strange. I looked away to see if she would stop. She didn't. I finally asked if there was anything that I could help her with she said nothing. I tried everything. I even said, 'That sure is something about Martha Stewart, isn't it?' There was no response. She just kept looking at me. I decided to get up from my seat in front of her and move down the car. The strange thing is her face did not change or move the whole time; she did not blink or move. I got up and moved; she just stared in the same spot as if I were still there." George sat there finishing his Coke off shaking his head.

"What happened next?" Angelica said mesmerized by this odd occurrence.

"I looked back down the aisle to see if there was any change. At first there was none; she just sat there fixated on that one spot; then all-of-a-sudden there was a blink. She began to shake and look as if she was waking up. There was a slight noise that came from her lips. I was too far down to hear what it was. She looked around like she was lost. She looked like she had been dreaming. There was something about this woman and her absence of mind that made me shiver. I can't tell you what she was thinking, but she looked confused."

"Maybe she had a catatonic episode. When one has something like that they freeze in time. It is a form of cataplexy." Dr. Williams sounded like she knew what she was talking about and like she had earned her degree. "Was there anything else?"

"No, the rest of the trip was ok she finally found her eyes back my way and just looked puzzled. After a bit, she looked back at her paper and began to read it again. My stop was approaching. I gathered my things and exited the subway car." George said.

"Anything else you can think of about your trip home?" The doctor asked.

"Nope, I got out of the subway and went up the street to my apartment building. I got my mail out of the box in the lobby. Nothing important, just bills. I went up the stairs to my apartment and opened the door. Everything from there was like normal."

"So from there you just went about you regular nightly routines?"

"Yep, I think so. If there was anything out of the ordinary, I didn't see it. I put the food in the fridge took a third shower for the day and went to bed." George poured more Coke in his cup.

"Well, did you not eat anything that night?" Angelica inquired while pouring Coke for herself.

"No come to think of it the peanuts at the bar kept me sustained for the night. I guess it is the high level of protein in the nuts."

"What was the time you went to bed?"

"I guess it was 12:30 or maybe a little later. I don't remember. I just went to bed. Come to think of it this was out of the ordinary because I am always conscious of what time I am off to bed."

The Interview

"I see." Dr. Williams wiped her mouth and picked up her pen to jot this little irregularity down.

Chapter 7

Yesterday

After finishing the pizza, Dr. Williams called Eddie in to get the remains and bring in a fresh pot of coffee and two new cups.

"Now we are up to the day of the murders…" Dr. Williams was interrupted.

"THEY WERE NOT MURDERS!" George yelled. "I DID NOT KILL THEM!"

"Ok then, George, this is where you just need calmly to tell me what happened, starting with that morning. What was the first thing you did when you woke up?"

"Are you done accusing me of these crimes?" He asked.

"I'm giving you the chance to tell me your story." Angelica began to sound soothing and sympathetic again. "Will you start with what happened when you got out of bed yesterday morning?"

"Ok, after the alarm went off, I jumped up and got to the bathroom. I took a piss and got into the shower. Is that what you wanted?" You could tell the tone of sarcasm in his voice.

Dr. Williams took her eyes off her pad and looked up, "Ok, SMART ASS. Now if you could tell me what you did next." Her tone switched from sympathetic to harsh and jagged.

"After I got out of the shower I brushed my teeth." He tried to give as much detail to be more of an ass. "I used the Colgate toothpaste because the other makes my teeth hurt."

"Ok, you can stop right there. Get over being mad at me and speak civilly to me or you can go to the dogs when you step in that courtroom tomorrow. Now tell me the important stuff."

"Well let's see. I went and made me some coffee and toasted a bagel to eat on the train ride to work. I grabbed a small pack of cream cheese to go and left. I got to the subway station as usual. I hopped on the next train and headed off to work. There was a morning paper someone had left in my seat, so I picked it up to begin to read it. I finished up my coffee and bagel while reading more on the Martha Stewart situation. There was also an interesting article on the price of gas. I thought that I would read the gas article while I was out to lunch. I put the paper under my arm and got off at my stop.

I walked a block to my building while thinking of some strange computer code I had seen

The Interview

the day before. When I got to the elevator, there was a large line, so I had to catch the next one. I was the first on the elevator, so I pressed 13 on the pad and went to the back. A whole car full of people crammed in front of me. The people shouted random numbers off '15, 12, 5, 13' no one had a higher number than me. This was a 22-floor building. The first stop was on the fifth floor. Two people got out there. I began to think on the ride as we passed floor 9, 10, and 12, about the date and how I screwed up. I got so caught up in thinking about the date I did not realize that no one was getting off on the floors that we stopped on. Next thing I know we are at my floor and the final stop and there are people just standing there. No other floors to go and no one getting off. I had to push my way through the crowd. No one would move when I said excuse me. Everyone just stared forward. The door started to close, and no one moved, so I just pushed through the crowd. They were just frozen like the woman on the subway the night before. When I pushed them, you would expect them to fall over like bowling pins but they were more like pliable figures. The door had shut completely by the time I made it to the front and the elevator just stood there motionless It did no godown or up or anything. I pressed the open door button to get out." George poured some coffee in his cup and took a sip.

"So this is the second time you have encountered people standing in place?" Angelica said. She thought it was strange that twice everyone in his presence had frozen. "What were their facial expressions when you looked at them?"

The Interview

"Yes this was the second time I have encountered frozen individuals... I know you think I'm crazy... But I'm not. Their faces were like any normal face just blank expressions. There was no feeling in any of the individuals on the elevator. I was the only one that seemed to be in this world." George sat up straight in his chair.

"Ok, after you left the elevator full of people what did you do?" Angelica inquired.

"I walked down the hall past Mr. Sweet's door. I got to the end of the hall and entered the floor of cubicles. I walked past mine and sat down. I went over the thing I had done the day before, in my head while I turned on my computer. I then took out a notepad and got ready to start on my next assignment." George rubbed his eyes as he told this as if he were getting sleepy from the food and drink.

"Why did you takeout a notepad?" Dr. Williams asked.

"I have to have it on my desk while I program. I need it to write the name of a line of code so that I may go back and reference. It's a practice that started back in college." George found a comfortable position for his eyes and stared. "Next I opened my email and began to read the background information on my new assignment. It seems that a program to track money lost some money, somewhere along the way. I found that when I placed the money in an account and transferred it to another account there was an eighth of a cent lost somewhere. Every eight transactions there was one cent lost. For a large banking firm that relied on this program to manage this account, it makes an audit nightmare."

"Did you know right away how to fix it?" Angelica asked.

"No, but I did know it was just in the transfers of classes." When he started to talk about classes and field names, Angelica zoned out. She shook her head making it seem that she knew what he was talking about. She knew nothing of programming of a computer. She thought to herself, 'I can program the mind.' Thinking of this made her laugh.

"What?" He asked.

"...What" Angelica stopped shaking her head. "I was thinking of programming and how I would suck at it." She shook her head in approval of the subject. "You go ahead and finish telling me how."

"Oh ok… Well, I'm almost there was just a wrong semicolon count. All I had to do was delete one of them, and the program ran fine. Just to make sure I created a test that simulated ten million transfers of one dollar. At the end of the simulated transfers, I had one dollar. I had fixed the problem. George sat up straight and sounded like he just had saved the day. He was so proud and looking for congratulations from his new doctor and friend, he found none.

"How can you look at multiple pages of code and determine what is wrong. How can you tell that the semicolon was not needed?" Angelica asked.

"It comes from doing it over and again, I guess." George looked like he was still looking for congratulations. "I did fix it though. No one that wrote the program realized that little problem. The compiler did not catch it. I did it on my own."

"How long did it take you to finish this problem? She asked."

"I got done around 9:30 it did not take me long to fix it. I'm just that good," George was still proud.

"I'm sure you are just that good." Angelica responded.

George had finally got some form of a response that he wanted. "Yeah... Next I started on a project for the US Military. It was a communication problem. The encryption was not translated properly."

"Sounds like you know your stuff, George." Angelica said.

"Yeah, I guess I do." Now that he got what he was fishing for he was satisfied.

-*Lunch Yesterday* she wrote on her pad.

"When in all this programming, did you stop to take lunch, George?" Angelica inquired.

"I stopped around 12:30 give or take 15 minutes." George grabbed his fist and started to tense up. He knows where the conversation is about to go. "I stopped thirty minutes before I was supposed to take my lunch. I did not want to get in the middle of the program and have to leave it. The lunch time is more of a guideline than an actual rule."

Angelica asked, "Did you notice anyone else taking lunch at that time?"

The Interview

"No, I just went to lunch when I finished the program I was on. There was no one going to lunch at the same time as me. After I finished I clocked out on the time clock interface linked through all computers in the building." George looked at her like a sad puppy.

"You do know Whitney went to lunch at about the same time, just thirty minutes earlier. Both lunches were about one-half hour overlapping. What I am trying to ask is did you plan this overlapping period?" Angelica dropped her Mont Blanc and sat up straight to take the blow he was about to give.

"No, I did not." George completely overturned Dr. William's original observation. He did not lash out or scream. He just said, "No, I did not." His face-stayed plain... "No, I did not. I did know until after I saw her down at the food stand."

"So you did go straight downstairs where you found Whitney at the hotdog stand?" Angelica noted his confusion and looked up again.

"No, when I entered the time in the computer I went to the restroom, I washed my hands, and then I headed to the elevator. As I went down I debated to go left to 5th street or right to the hotdog stand. It was a matter of money. I had very little yesterday, so I went to the hotdog stood where there were hotdogs and polish sausages for a buck-fifty." George by this time was visibly agitated. He balled his fist together and slammed them on the table. "I DID NOT INTENTIONALLY GO TO THE HOTDOG STAND TO SEE HER!"

The Interview

When George slammed his fist on the table, he startled Dr. Williams; she jumped back in her seat. "What is this anger for George?"

"You are trying to make just a coincidence into something that it's not. I did not go after her on this day we meet at the hotdog stand. When I saw her there, I froze. I thought should I still go and eat there because there she was standing there ordering her hotdog and Coke." The tension in him was finally relaxing making Angelica relax more too. "I decided to go to the hotdog stand and get my lunch. Then I planned to go across the street to the park to eat it.

"I watched her get her hotdog and take a seat on the bench on the sidewalk. She did not see me. I went to the corner of the stand to try and avoid her, and to order my food. I ordered a polish dog all the way, with onions and green peppers. She did not notice me. I then ordered a Dr. Pepper and paid."

"What if any interaction did you have with her?" Angelica noted the differences in what they ordered.

"At first I stood there and waited. I went through this in my head. I thought, 'Can I fix what I've done?' She was just sitting there eating. I thought to myself I would just apologize and see if we can just remain friends." George placed his hands flat on the table and sighed.

"Angelica in her most understanding voice said, "Its ok George."

"Easy for you to say you did not see what happened next. I went to the edge of the hotdog stand and watched her for a second." George picked up his hands. He held them in front of his face so that his eyes were covered completely. "I started to walk forward she had just finished her food. She looked up and saw me. Right then when our eyes meet I saw something in her. I saw anger. I wanted to stop her. I wanted her to stop what she was doing and just listen to me. She didn't stop." George slammed his hands on the table again. He shook his head and began to weep in pain. He began to cry like someone had just killed his dog. Angelica could read a sense of remorse in his pain. "She got up and said what I believe to be her last words. She sat her drink down on the bench where she was just sitting. The anger in her eyes was intense. She said 'I don't want to talk to you.' She was angry. 'Just go away' she said. I told her that I just wanted to talk to her.

She turned to walk in the other direction I spoke loud and clear 'Please stop, I just want to be friends.' She acted like she did not hear me and continued to walk on. I took two steps when I realized something was wrong. I looked to my right and saw a bus out of the corner of my eye just past the hotdog stand going fast. Then I saw Whitney veering to the sidewalk. My heart stopped, and I began to sprint. Just as I took my first foot off of the ground, and my heart started back she paused in mid walk right on the edge of the crosswalk. I looked, and the bus was within six feet of her. I was within three. I just made the grab for her arm when she was struck. The bus slammed on its brakes."

George rubbed the sweat from his face and eyes. "I could not help but look at the people staring and thinking that the last thing she ever thought of me was how mad she was at me for what I said."

"Wow George, this is a lot to digest." Dr. Williams wrote vigorously on her yellow note pad. "Just give me a minute to jot down some notes." As she wrote, George began to dry up the tears he had formed telling his story.

"So what you are saying is that you were trying to save her."

George replied promptly. "Yes of course I was trying to save her. No matter what had happened I cared for her. It was another incident again where she just froze. Like the people on the elevator."

Chapter 8

Meeting with the Boss

"So... What happened next?" Angelica asked. "Did you stick around to cry over the body or did you leave?"

"I left... I was in shock..." George felt like he had to defend himself. He felt like she was making fun of him. "I went back to the building."

"What was going through your mind while you were walking to the building?"

"All I could think about was how she just froze. I yelled for her to stop, and she did. Like the people in the elevator did. I don't know how this is happening." George stretched out his hands and looked very concerned. "I just went back to the building. Nothing went through my mind, except how could this be happening.

When I got back inside, I went to the elevator and pressed the button. There were many people around me looking up at what floor the elevator was on. I was thinking the whole time about the event that had just happened. I never even noticed at the time that everyone stayed off of the elevator. I got in and pressed my button, and looked up just as the door closed. When I looked up I saw as the door was closing that no one had gotten in and that everyone was still standing outside looking up at the Floor that the elevator was on. I guess that no one knew that they were on floor one unless the needle broke that told the floor location of the elevator.

After this, I began to theorize about the condition of the people outside. They all seemed comatose or catatonic. I began at this point to put two and two together. I was having an effect on the actions of other people."

144

"What do you mean, having an effect?" Dr. Williams asked.

"Well, I just told you. I told her to stop, and she did halfway on the sidewalk and half way on the street. I told her to do it. She did it. I made it happen. She was still for at least one, or a good one and a half seconds. Enough time went past for everything to process through my mind that she was about to be hit by that bus.

When I got inside and looked at the floor, and thought how she just stopped and looked frozen. I got on the elevator and looked up everyone was frozen looking at the floor indicator. Other people outside the circle of statues was moving. I don't know how it happened, but it did."

"Ok then go on and tell me more about what happened when you got off the elevator." Angelica, thinking as a doctor, was beginning to think he was crazy. She knew that no one was capable of controlling the actions of humans. She thought his sense of grandeur could be some kind of Schizophrenia or bipolar episode.

George moved in his seat and wrinkled his brow. "Ok... When I got to the floor that I work on, I just go back to my seat and begin to read the emails that piled up while I was out causing a death."

Angelica interrupted. "You say that you are the cause of the death of Whitney?"

"No, that's not what I'm saying. All that I am saying is that there was something that happened between us that caused her to pause for that split second that lead to her demise. I can't express how it happened I yelled out for her to stop, and she did but not like a person should stop. It was in mid walk. She had one foot on the sidewalk and one off."

"Ok then, you did not push her though." She said

"No..." He replied.

"Tell me more about returning and reading your emails." Angelica wrote this incident down that he still proclaims his innocence.

"Well, I got one from my boss saying that he needed to see me before I left for the day. I responded by saying just come get me when he was ready. I got an email saying I needed to turn in something to marketing for approval. By the time I replied to this Mr. Sweet's secretary had come over and said 'Mr. Sweet will see you now.' I got up and followed her to his office down next to the

The Interview

elevators. I walked through his doors and Mrs. Lynch, his secretary, closed the doors behind me.

'George my main man, how's it hang-in?' he said in the most southern accent. He has tried to become my friend, but I just don't like the man. He asked me to sit down, I did. Then he started to ask me how much I liked the current position I was in. I told him I liked what I did and that I was good at it. He told me, 'Yeah you have caught things that would have resulted in a multimillion dollar lawsuit. Thanks to you we stay in the profit margin.' I just took all of this as a compliment and him trying to get me to like him again.

He quickly changed the subject with, "You know I like my job. I like my job until I have to do what I'm about to do.' My stomach went into my feet. I thought he was about to fire me."

"He did not fire you at this point?" Dr. Williams asked.

"No. He just said that there had been a report filed on me, and he had to investigate both sides of the argument. He proceeded to ask a bunch of bullshit questions. I answered them with a yes and no response. All that was about was to see if there was a mental defect somewhere in my brain. There was none, so he began to ask if I knew some of the people in the office and what my relationship was with them. In most cases I answered, strictly professional or personal. He then came to Whitney and asked about her. I told him it was not a relationship anymore. And he continued to ask about some other people. I knew he was trying to avoid coming right out and pinpointing one person."

The Interview

"I think you are right. He was trying to avoid the obvious." Angelica tried to sound concerned and listening. She was taking notes vigorously. She tried not to interrupt too often he was on a roll, and she did not want to destroy the fluent motion of his talking.

"He said after this course of questioning. 'Like I said there has been a report made against you I will tell you what this whole thing is about now. But I need to record your response. What was the situation that happened between you and Whitney yesterday? Did you approach her in the workplace in any way?' I told him that I had gone up to her and asked her out and that she had agreed for later that night. I told him that was all that happened in the work place.

"Was that all that happened in the workplace?" Angelica asked.

"Hell yes, I told you all this already."

"I'm sorry I just needed to ask."

"Well, that's what I told him anyway. He then told me that she had come to him and filed a harassment case against me. I told him it was purely false. There was not anything even resembling harassment. 'She said you had been sending her emails saying you had threatened her to go out with you. She said that the only reason she went out with you was because she did not want you to do the thing she said you would do to her.' He tells me.

I was outraged. I told him that there had been no such emails and that she was crazy. There was nothing that I would ever do to her if she didn't go out with me. I loved that girl. I told Mr. Sweet that he could pull up the email conversations and that there was nothing going on between us now. He said 'Of course not now that she has filed this report.'

Mr. Sweet told me to go home with pay and let him process the report and make an investigation."

"That sounds like a good deal to me George." Angelica stated.

"All I did then is to tell him that there was no need to process the paperwork because she no longer felt that way. Mr. Sweet sat up in his seat to look at me closer and said, 'How can you possibly know how she feels now?' I proceeded to tell him that simply while she was out to lunch there was an accident. He stood up out of his seat and said, 'What did you do to her, George.'

"Nothing... What do you mean?"

"Is she ok?" Mr. Sweet sat back down in his desk.

"Well, I don't think so...." George began to look down at his feet.

"What has happened, George?" Mr. Sweet sounded concerned.

George thought about the reply to this for a few seconds. He tried to plan a route to less conflict, but he had to tell him. "What happened to her today, George?"

"Well, Mr. Sweet let's just say she is in medical custody; being treated by the best." George after thinking about his response felt a little more confidant and looked away from his feet.

The Interview

Mr. Sweet stood up from his chair and with the backs of his calves pushed the chair to the edge of the window seal. He stood perched behind his desk with his arms grinding into the wood. "WHAT DID YOU DO TO HER GEORGE?"

"Stop yelling Mr. Sweet. I didn't do anything to her…" George cowered down in his seat. "Stop yelling…"

Mr. Sweet took is right fist and slammed it into the desk. "What happened George? What did you do to her?"

"You know Dr. Williams there was a time during this conversation where I got really scared. I thought I was going to cry sitting there watching him slam his fist on the desk and yell at the top of his lunges. After this sudden rush of being frightened he stopped." George said.

"What do you mean he stopped, George?" Angelica asked.

"He just stopped. I thought of first he was doing it because my pleas to stop, but it was more. He was frozen. He froze like the people at the elevator and like Whitney on the street."

"What do you think the 'frozen' people mean?" Dr. Williams asked. "Well, never mind George." Dr. Williams realized he was still unsure about the mysterious freezing people as he was. "Never mind George; what happened next?"

"Well, I went to the door and started to leave when I thought I heard him move. I turned around to see him in-fact standing still frozen. I thought for sure I was losing it, so I went over to just touch him to see if he was still alive. He was

The Interview

frozen in mid-sentence. I have never seen someone with such an expression on his face before.

I started to approach him, and his facial expression changed, startling me and causing me to take one step back from my target. Everything went through my mind trying to figure what was causing everyone that I have been around to freeze. I thought it was my mind freezing me while time was wondering on. But that made no logical sense. I can't figure it out.

Back to what I was saying; I went to take another step forward and nothing happened. I got within three feet from Mr. Sweet when I thought I had frozen. I just stood there three feet away from him staring at him breathing. All I could do is wonder what had caused this. I stuck my hand out to touch him to see if there was something wrong. I held my hand out with my index finger extended inching closer to him. I got a millimeter from him and he jumped. That jump scared me so much that I yelled out the first thing that came to mind. I was so frightened. Then just as he had been awakened he went to sleep again, so to speak.

I stood there for another five minutes or so watching him in an utterly frozen state. I turned and walked out. I turned to Mr. Sweets secretary and said 'Mr. Sweet doesn't want to be disturbed.

Mr. Sweet's secretary is named Rachel and was hired on with me. She had been a loyal friend for years. She said 'I'm so sorry to hear about this George.' She then hands me a light baby blue envelope with **Confidential** spelled out in bold black letters. I told her 'thank you' and walked out of the office."

The Interview

"I have a couple of questions for you George." Dr. Williams said.

"Ok shoot" He quickly replied.

"What was in the envelope?"

"Well, it was my termination papers effective the next day from Mr. Sweet. I guess that's why he called me to his office. I opened the envelope when I left his office. Then I remembered there being a pink copy of this slip on his desk."

"One last thing George; when you were in the office, about to touch him, what were you thinking?"

"Well, I guess I thought I was going to wake him up, but he scared me." George said.

What did you yell out when he scared you? You said you said the first thing that came to mind, what was that?"

"Well, this is going to sound bad considering the circumstances." He replied.

"It's ok George."

"Well, my exact words were 'Go jump off a bridge, fuck head.'."

Chapter 9

Blast from the past

"What happened next, George?" Angelica inquired. "What happened when you left the office?" She was into the story now and stopped analyzing him. She got out of the chair and stretched. She poured more coffee for her and George.

"Well, I just began thinking of all the things I had gone through in that office. I began to notice how everyone was looking at me. It seemed that everyone knew already. The whole office looked at me when I returned to my desk... Thank you for the coffee, Dr. Williams." George took the coffee in one hand and took a sip. He made a slurping noise when he sipped his coffee. "This is good coffee, isn't it?"

The Interview

"Yes it is George. What did you think about while you were collecting your things from your desk?" Dr. Williams took a sip of her coffee. There was no noise when she took a drink. George noticed and decided not to make a noise he next time he drank.

"When I got back to the desk I thought back on my life. I wondered if there had ever been a situation where I had ever felt worse."

"Well, was there a situation where you had felt worse?" Angelica took another sip off coffee. No noise.

"Yeah, there is just one other time in my life where I felt worse. Not even the death of my parents can top this experience." Dr. Williams noted the death of his parents on her paper. George began, "It was back in high school. I went to Cass

Comprehensive High. There was a large group of friends that I hung out with. I had an incident with them that was worse than what I went through yesterday. I think that was the only time in my life. If that is, there was another time I can't remember." George paused to take another sip of coffee. No noise.

"What happened to you George?" Angelica asked.

"What happened that summer is buried now. We don't need to dig it up." George took another soundless sip of his coffee.

"George, this thing that happened in your past, may have some relevance to the case, and in my decision in diagnosing you. This thing in your past may have been something out of your control. Just give me a shot with this I may even be able to help you cope with the situation. That's my job you know..."

"Ok. Ok. I'll tell you if you stop babbling."

"Thank you George." She replied.

"There is a cemetery in the town I grew up in called Oak Hill. As kids, we were sacred of this cemetery. No one wanted to get near it after dark. It was the kind that was over a hundred years old and had lots of old tombstones and crypts. This place was at least a hundred acres or more. We all went in there during the day to just play around and see if anyone could conjure up some spirits or something. This was a large cemetery with miles and miles of graves and of course oak trees. This one had, for some strange reason, a large fence around it, and big cast iron gates that had huge locks on them. We all guessed that it was to keep the vandals out at night. The local police department closed the gates every night and locked them. There was even a sign as you went into the gate that said 'Gate Closes at Dusk.' There were always stories on how they locked them at night to keep the ghouls and goblins in."

"Sounds scary George," the doctor observed.

"Yeah, it was a frightening place. I had many nightmares about that place as a child. There were some friends of mine that talked about going on the grounds after dark. The sign on the inside gate read 'Gate Closes at Dusk.' There was no reason to go in, in my opinion.

One night after a football game the three of them asked me if I wanted to catch a late flick with them. Of course, I said, yeah, recognizing their popularity. On the way to the movies, we had to pass by the cemetery. It was still daylight then, and there was a good hour till dusk so they decided to drive through the cemetery. I was ok with it because I was only frightened at night. We drove through and around the bin to where I recognized the plot where my great-grandfather was buried. We drove to the other side where the other entrance was; there are only two entrances to the cemetery. We drove out and went to the theater.

When we got out of the movie, we went back to the school where all of the passenger cars were parked. I remembered looking up at the sky that night. I looked up in that open convertible at the beautiful moon. There was the largest most beautiful full moon that night.

When we made it back to the gate, it had been left open. The guys wanted to go in to be one of the only few to have bragging rights to the whole going in at dark thing. It had been dark for about an hour and thirty minutes now. I agreed with them just to not be the only one to be a bore or a party pooper, you know. Peer pressure can do marvelous things you know." He took another drink of coffee with no slurping sounds.

"Yes George I do know the power of peer pressure." Angelica drank more coffee and said, "Go on what happened when you got in there."

"Well, nothing we got to the other side and the gate was closed, so we decided to go back around the long way to get out of the place. We got to side we had entered, and there was a police car pulling out of the place with a locked Gate. He must have been locking the other side while we entered this side. And when we took the long way around he locked the only other entrance and exit to the place."

"Oh my god, George," Angelica said.

"Yeah, we were in some deep shit. I was about to die of fright. Here we were in a cemetery at night with two locked gates and a twenty-foot tall brick fence. I didn't know what to do. Everyone around me tried to act cool, but it was obvious that they were scared shitless. The sign on the other side of the gate read gate opens at dawn and closes at dusk. All we could do is pace outside the car and yell at each other about whose fault this whole thing was.

I said to the other guys, 'we need to stop blaming each other and devise a plan to get out of here. There is no good going to come out of yelling at each other.' After I said this, we decided to walk the fences' perimeter and find some way of getting over it."

"How did that go? There must have been some animosity still in the group." Angelica asked.

"There was some hostility still among us but we all left anyway to find a way out. We left the car at the gate so that if anyone were to pass by the road they would hopefully look for the people the car belonged to.

Although we thought this would be a good idea, we soon found that there was a little light and a long ways to walk. There were several times where we all had to stop to check out if we could climb a tree to get to the top and over the fence. The trip had to have been six or seven miles around the perimeter. We only found one promising spot where we could have had a chance to get over. The bricks as I said were twenty foot tall from the inside. Where we found a spot where a crypt and a tree helped us climb to the top of the fence. When we got to the top, we looked down to find the twenty-foot drop and another thirty-food cliff.

There was nowhere to go. We walked the rest of the perimeter back to the car and began to panic. Ron, the guy that owned the car, took it and slammed it into the Iron Gate resulting in a busted front end. The gate sustained no damage. This was the moment where we realized that the gate was meant to keep someone in and not vandals out. There were several points in the night where we were convinced that we were not getting out alive."

What happened during the night that would convince you that you would not get out alive? This situation sounds like there are some conditions of the night that were dangerous." Angelica pointed out.

"Oh yeah, there were. There were many things that happened to us before we blacked out."

Dr. Williams jotted down many things in her notes while asking questions. "You blacked out? How do you mean?"

"Well, about half way through the night I can't remember anything that happened. I lost about a week. I woke up in the hospital, or came to is more like it. My parents were there and said that I lay there all week in bed with my eyes open. The doctors described it as a type of catatonia."

"Wow… so tell me what happened that you can remember?" Dr. Williams was still writing this whole time on her pad.

The Interview

"Well, where do I start? I guess from when we got back from our long walk around the perimeter. We got back in the car and began to ram it again. I guess we rammed the gate another four times before the power died, and the headlights went out. Shortly after we got out of the car it began to smoke. I guess it was from the steam coming out of the radiator. I told the guys that we must have busted it ramming the gate.

We all just stood there next to the car and tried to figure out what to do next. Dustin asked me for the time. I was the only one there that had a wrist watch. It was midnight. We all could not believe it had gotten that late. We also realized that we had just broken the car at the gate on a road least traveled. We also came to the realization that this one-horse town closes down at eleven o'clock.

The only store that even stayed open that extra two hours was Wal-Mart. I lived in a very small Podunk town that even today Wal-Mart closes early. I think it is the only Wal-Mart in the company that isn't open 24-hours."

"So you were stuck, for the night that is." Dr. Williams observed.

"Yep, we didn't get out until the gates opened by the police six hours later. I can only remember about another hour though. This was the longest hour of the night it seemed that we were in there for six days inside of that one-hour. It was like we had entered a time warp inside of the Oak Hill Gates.

We all stood outside the car planning our next course of action. We all agreed that once we returned to school on Monday that we would be famous not that we had accepted that we were to spend the night in there. I must have been the only one in the group that thought this was not a cool thing. But I guessed that this type of thing is what made these boys so popular. I was truly scared shitless. My stomach was doing cartwheels. Dustin the leader of our posse said we should roam the cemetery and look around. So we did, and this is where things begin to go wrong."

"Wrong, how so?" the good doctor interjected.

"Well, just sit back and keep your mind open. This gets choppy and weird. You know I told you that the cemetery was named Oak Hill right?" Dr. Williams nodded "Well it consisted of many hills with Oak trees covering the hills. The graves were arranged on the hill on built up leveled off spots. Rock walls held up these plot areas. From the bottom of the hill, it looked like a short fat pyramid. To get to the top of the hill you had to cross many large grave plot areas. Many people on these hills erected large monuments and tombs above ground. And also many people just were buried with a large marker stone or headstone.

We all decided to take a walk up the first-hill close to the entrance of the gate. We started up stopping to look at some names on the graves also to look at dates. We had a decent time going through the plots looking at names. We got to some areas that that were very educational.

Close to the top but not quite to the top we noticed graves got older, much older. The one that made us stop and reflect for a while was a grave with no name just a year of death and the cause of death. The headstone very simply read here lies the female witch hanged 1799 at Oak hill cemetery.'."

Dr. Williams took her eyes off here paper for this one and stared blankly at George. "Yeah, it creeps you out too huh? Here we are stuck at a place used not only to bury the people of the town, but also used to hang the criminals.

Everyone looked at each other shrugged it off and began to climb to the top of the hill. This particular hill was the oldest and largest with a very old oak tree at the top. We continued to the top looking at the stones on the way up we saw many more and criminals and witch trial stones. We also passed on the way to the top a large obelisk labeled here lies Judge Jones 1810. I thought it was kind of strange all of these people sentenced to death by Judge Jones surround him on the hilltop he laid.

After what seemed like an hour we finally reached the top and Dustin asked for the time again. I looked at my watch, and it hadn't moved. It still read 12 o'clock. Dustin just cursed my peace of shit watch. I couldn't figure it out; it was a new watch I had just gotten for my birthday. So we were timeless and didn't know what would happen next. From the top of the hill, we could see many other hills like this one throughout the cemetery. All were smaller than this one. We all sat on the ground under the great Oak tree of the cemetery. Joe pointed out that this is where many of those people we passed on the way up had been hanged. We all had a full body cold chill come over us.

The Interview

At the top of this hill is where we found a little glimmer of hope. We could see most of the cemetery well the full moon lit most of the grounds. There was this large area in the rear next to the far wall that was dark. Now I'm not talking a shadow over the area I'm talking D.A.R.K. dark. Dustin noticed this area first and pointed out that someone was down there. Whoever was in this dark portion of the cemetery had a light. It looked like an old lantern for mining or something we could not make a person out because of how dark it was. He would have looked like an ant anyway.

Dustin yells at the top of his lungs down to a glimmer of light, 'Hey you there we need help.' There was no response no one yelled back, but the light seemed to move to the right some as if moving from one grave to another. We all agreed that someone else must have been trapped in for the night as well. So we began to run and run quick. The one or two miles from the hilltop down through the valleys between the hills alone the curvy roadways to the darker portion of the cemetery. Once we started to approach the dark portion we noticed it getting darker. Like the darkness started to expand to meet us on the way to the man. All while running we all were yelling at him to help us "Hey you there Sir.' The man did not turnaround as we got within a football field's length of him we all stopped. We were inside the darkness now, and the man appeared to be digging.

'Hey, you dude can you help us?' Dustin just yells out at the man. I told the group that I thought he is a grounds keeper, and that he was digging a grave. The man was dressed in blue jean overalls with a dingy shirt under them. He looked as if he had a hunch in his back from doing this job for many years. He wore old leatherwork boots with the laces undone on them. He also had a lantern made of cast iron on a large hooked stick stuck in the ground next to the grave. He had a large shovel and dug one scoop at a time.

We all looked at each other and noticed that about a hundred yards from him was a stone hut with one-window and a door, and there was a light on inside. We all agreed that this was the grounds keeper and chief gravedigger. And the hut with the light on was his office of-sorts. Dustin told us that we needed to go talk to the gravedigger and see if we could use the phone in his hut. I objected and said that we needed just to go to the hut and use the phone this man wants nothing to do with us obviously, or he would have answered us by now.

Dustin, the apparent group leader just, said 'Look dude he is obviously an old man and just can't hear us. He will understand once we get closer and tell him our story. Now come on we can't do anything until we go talk to him. I know he will help us.' So we all walked the short distance to the grave keeper. As we approached the man, we noticed he must have been working for some time. There were three graves he had dug in a row, and he had just begun on his fourth.

We finally got up to him to see his face and if you didn't find him creepy yet you will now. He was old, and I'm talking late 50's to a teenager this was ancient. His face pale his hair was, long, stringy, and grey. It looked as if he hadn't washed it in a couple of years. Dustin said in a loud voice 'Sir; we got locked in here tonight. Can we use the phone in your hut to call our parents to come get us?' The caretaker just kept digging as if he hadn't heard a thing. I remember the sound of the dirt sending chills up my back as his shovel sliced into the earth.

Dustin, getting a little frustrated, goes over and stands in the grave in front of the gravedigger. I yelled over to say I don't think that's such a good idea. He lowered his head to say 'can you hear me?' The man didn't flinch he just dug more and more. Dustin then taps him on his forehead and said 'I know you can see me dude. What the fuck is wrong with you?' When there was no response from the man digging, I suggested we just go over to the hut and call he obviously didn't give a shit that we were there.

We left the man to his digging and walked to the hut where the light was shining bright inside. Before we went inside we looked in the only window in the hut. Joe had to wipe the dust off so that he could see in. it was like a little house there was a fireplace with a fire burning, a cot to sleep on, and a little kitchen area with a sink a mirror and toilet. There was no one inside, so we let ourselves in. there was a strange musty smell as we went into the hut. There was no phone that we could see and no other doors or windows.

We started to look around to notice the little details of the hut." Dr. Williams flipped the page over and began writing on a new page. She also picked up the recorder to make sure it was still recording. "We noticed things like the wood next to the fireplace and books on the table. The books we found were strange. There was a textbook on human anatomy and books on autopsies.

While examining the books, we found a critical item under them. It was a newspaper that was dated in 1801 and looked like a new paper though. We were paralyzed in fear to what we saw on the front page. Dustin dropped the autopsy book on the floor to give a loud bang. We all jumped at this noise. 'No fucking way. There is no goddamn way.' Dustin yelled out. On the cover of the paper was a picture of us. All four of us were pictured on the front. Also, there was a title equally disturbing. I will never forget it 'Sentenced to hang'."

"Wow…. That would scare me to death. What else did it say?" Dr. Williams asked while pouring more coffee.

"Well, here's the thing. It said that Judge Jones the grave we passed on the top of the hill had convicted us of Loitering, Breaking and Entering, and this is the kicker vandalizing the Oak Hill Cemetery with some unknown horseless buggy contraption. As I read this aloud to the group, our jaws dropped. The paper stated that we were to be hanged at dawn of that very day only in 1801.

Now Doctor, just sit back, there is more unbelievable shit. We all started pacing the small hut cursing all sorts of obscenities. As you can understand, after seeing that paper were scared to death. Johnny who was the quieter one of the group pointed out that there were four graves that man

The Interview

was digging and that there were exactly four of us.
We all paused and looked at one another. Shaking
my head in disbelief, for whatever reason, I finally
looked at my watch again. It was 12:15 only fifteen
minutes had passed since we had left the car.
Dustin just said that my watch was just slow the
battery had gone dead.

As we were pondering over the battery in
my watch and wondering what to do next, the door
to the hut opened. It was a man digging the graves.
In the most horrifying voice, something like how
the crypt keeper on that show, Tales from the
Crypt, would say it. 'You boys don't go too far now.
The plots are almost ready for you. The dawn is
coming, just you boys wait.' Then came the cackle.
It would have sent chills up the back of an infant. As
he made this horrifying cackle with his green teeth

showing we all at once pushed the old man out of the way and ran out the door. As we ran, we could hear that horrible cackle in the background echoing through the cemetery.

We ran and ran until we couldn't run anymore, and we were all out of breath. Huffing and puffing gasping for air. Joe said, 'What the fuck. What the hell is going on here? Judge Jones' grave is at the top of that goddamn hill, what the fuck are we going to do.' By this point, I have to admit we all were shaking and scared for our life. 'We have to go somewhere so we can think.' Dustin told the group. So we went behind the nearest crypt and sat down to catch our breath and think about what to do next."

"Whoa... Whoa... Whoa...." Dr. Williams started in. "What you are telling me is that your face was on the paper. The paper dated 1801

right?"

"Yeah, that's right. Our face shot, or mug

shot if you will. It was drawn but an exact likeness

to all four of us. Under the picture was our name.

We knew that something was going on. Even if this

was a prank, and it would have been a damn good

one, how would someone know that by chance we

would drive through after the movies? It was an

impossible scenario."

"So you guys just ran out of the grave

keepers hut and stopped behind a crypt? If you ask

me, this sounds somewhat strange."

George sighed. "So you don't believe me?"

"I do but it's hard to believe that this

actually happened. If you say, it did then, I have no

other choice, but to believe you. Did the other guys

see the same thing in exactly the same way you did?" Dr. Williams returned to the notepad and began to jot some things down.

"Yes we all told the police afterward the same thing." George took another drink of coffee. This time he forgot and made a slurping noise. He realized it once he heard it and tried to correct it mid sip.

"Well then, what did you do next after you guys stopped behind the crypt?" As she spoke, she changed the tape in the recorder and flipped to a new page on her note pad.

"Next we just talked and tried to calm down. Joe started to breath really hard and took out his inhaler to calm his breathing. I asked the guys if they just experienced what I just did. Dustin said, 'You have to be shitting me. Was that really us

on the paper?' I just said yeah I think so.

Dustin told the group that we had to find some way

out of here before dawn came. I, of course, agreed

to this and just wondered how. I asked what the

group thought we should do to escape the walls of

the cemetery. No one had an idea on how we could

do that. The car had been busted at one of the gates.

We had walked the perimeter of the grounds and

found no way out without killing ourselves.

John said, 'We can't just sit here all night

let's get up and walk around and keep moving so

that creep can't find us.' I agreed with this and

suggested that we go to the top of one of those hills

to keep an eye on that grounds keeper. We all

agreed with this, so we started up the nearest hill.

We did not take the time to read stone names

190

because of how creeped-the-fuck out we were. I can only say that once we got to the top I thought we would have some sort of relief from the situation. That wasn't the case.

Once we reached the top of this hill there was one of those big oak trees we all stood under. We immediately located the man digging a grave with his lantern next to him. The grounds keeper was shoulder high in that fourth and final grave. We watched for a good while until we saw him throw out the shovel. It landed on the mound of dirt next to the last grave.

The old man climbed out and appeared to stretch and moan. We all stood single file next to one another watching him and only him. Then there it was again. That hell sent laugh. He was cackling again. Cackling while looking straight at us his finger extended toward us. He then took his pointed finger and slowly pointed to the neighboring hilltop. There

at the top of the hill was a crowd of people standing under the tree. There was one man in front of them all wearing a large black robe. He was dressed in a judge's robe.

The next thing we saw was horrifying. It was Joe being dragged kicking and screaming to the noose. We all gasped and looked at one another to only discover that Joe was missing." George then adjusted in his seat and cleared his throat. "Dr. Williams make no mistake as sure as I am standing here today that was Joe on that other hill top kicking and screaming."

"Ok, hold on a minute. I thought you told me that you all had the same story to tell the police."

Dr. Williams sounded a bit on the confused side. "So if Joe was to be hanged here how does he tell the police this story?"

"Joe told the same story up until this point he even described them dragging and him yelling for help. He couldn't remember any more after that point though. His memory of the experience stopped there. The three of us that was left recalled the event after that, but his blackout started there."

"Ok then... I guess continue." She said with a sigh

"We all witnessed them wrap the noose around his neck and pull him up high on one of the branches. He shook like a fish on a lure. After about a minute he stopped shaking and just as quick as we had seen him appear among the crowd yelling

The Interview

we saw him vanish off of the noose and off of the hilltop entirely.

We all looked around to see if he had all of a sudden joined us, but no it was only Dustin, John, and I left on our hilltop. The next thing I can remember is that fucking cackle ripping through the air again. We all looked back to the grave site again to see the man who dug the graves in the first place laughing and filling the first grave in. 'Oh my god. Oh my god. Oh, my fucking god... Joe is dead. Dustin spoke for the whole group with that one.

WheeeHeeHeeHeeHeeeeeeee ripped through the air of the night sky as he filled in the grave where Joe must have been. With that last laugh, we all in unison turned to run. We ran as fast as we could without stopping at the gate opposite where are car was. Without hesitation, we began to beat on the gate yelling for someone to save us. I mean we were beginning to go horse we were yelling so much. I found a loose brick on the column holding one side of the Iron Gate up. I grabbed it and began to beat it against the iron making a clanking noise. All the while we were hearing the echo of the gravedigger.

We all began to wear down as the adrenalin flow began to slow. I rested my head against the gate and began to pant from fear. 'We are not going to get out of here alive are we?' Dustin asked. My response was just I don't think so…

As we rested against the gate hoping that someone would pass by to yell at when we heard a voice. This was a new voice. It was a grungy smoker's voice. It was very deep and robust. 'Hey boys you're a-goanna be late for the next hanging.' We look over to the column where I had pulled the brick from was. There is the judge figure from the other hilltop was standing there. He placed his green-tinted hand with long yellow fingernails on my shoulder. He had a greenish tint to the leather skin on his face. His robe was all dusty and musty smelling. It was like he had just been dug up for this freak show. We all jumped back and began to scramble.

I did the only thing I could think of at the time." Dr. Williams readjusted in her seat as to be getting anxious. "I yelled out at the group to follow me. I ran to the next hill to find something to hide behind. I could tell that this hill was closer to the gravedigger than the gate was because we could hear his laughter getting louder, that horrible cackle. I found a rather large crypt to hide behind.

It was a family crypt or a mausoleum; I can never tell the difference. The name over the stone door read DEVOROUX. The only thing I could think if at this point was to get inside.

The door was solid stone with Iron hinges holding it to the rest of the building. There was a latch mechanism that held the door closed. I finally figured out to twist the handle so that it unlocked the door from inside (there were two rods that held the door closed when you twist the handle on the outside the rods drew inwards and allowed you to open the door).

Once we reached the inside of the crypt I did a quick look around inside, there were two-stone sarcophagi on the floor. One had the bust of a lady on the top and the other had the bust of a man. Right before I closed the door behind us John yelled

The Interview

'Wait.' I turned to look to see that John was standing between the two sarcophaguses alone. 'Where is Dustin?' he asked. I then realized that he must not have followed me. Instead of shutting the door, I looked out to see if I could see Dustin. He was nowhere in sight. I stepped out, and no one was in sight. Not the judge not anyone.

Of course, we still heard the occasional laughter from the man filling in the grave (By this time he must have been done). We decided not to lock ourselves in the crypt but to go out and find our *apparent group leader*. We found that going to the top of that hill was the best way to spot him. On the way up we could see the man who had filled in the grave standing there with his lantern, grinning an evil grin. I looked at John and said 'What if they have Dustin now.' He just responded with a sigh.

After walking a couple more steps, John had a somewhat good idea. 'Let's go to the other side of this hill to see if they have him on the hanging hill.' I agreed rather than spend all of our time climbing to the top. Sure enough, we started around the base, and there was someone hanging on the noose looking very similar to Dustin. He was already dead; we had missed the show while in the crypt. The deed was done. As before the boy on the noose vanished, and just as before we heard that horrid laugh start up again. The man who once dug four graves was filling in his second one.

It happened to John the same way, and I was the last one. There was nowhere to run and nowhere to hide. We were just picked out of thin air and hanged then buried. The cops that opened the gate went looking for us when they saw the busted car. They found us all under that great oak tree covered in Georgia red clay. We were all unconscious. We were taken to the medical center in town and monitored until we were awake. We woke up in the order that we were taken, and all had the same story to tell the police.

So I think you will think twice before asking me what was going through my mind again."

"No George I won't, this was quite a helpful story. Did you relive the whole thing before you left your desk with your box of stuff?"

"Nope… I was just comparing what had just happened to me to that incident. That night in the graveyard is still on the top of that *worst things ever list*. I gathered my stuff in my XEROX paper box and walked to the elevator to go home.

Chapter 10

Video

"Dr. Williams," Sam burst in breathing heavy. "I need you in the next room, please."

Angelica forgot all about asking what happened to George's parents and stood up as to leave the room.

"Dr. Williams don't forget what we were talking about when you comeback. Ok?" George said she nodded and left the room with Sam.

Once in the hall just outside the interrogation room Dr. Williams paused and grabbed Sam's shoulder. "What is it Sam?"

"Well, we have the video of the subway it is very interesting. It seems as if he didn't push the guy in the subway. You just have to see this video."

"Ok let's go then." Dr. Williams and Sam went into the adjoining *mirror room*. Once on the inside there was a flat Sony television set with a paused image of the subway station on it. Once

The Interview

inside the room she also noticed the Assistant District Attorney, she recognized him from the courtrooms she had been in as a professional witness. She couldn't remember his last name but remembered the first *John*. There was also Eddie, the police officer that gave her the creeps standing there.

"Dr. Williams look at this and tell me if you have any insight on what is happening here." Sam walked over and pressed play on the remote.

Dr. Williams watched in amazement as she witnessed what was on the video. As she watched, there was an apparent image of George carrying his box of office supplies down the stairs. Once he was out of the frame the video switched to a scene of the staging area where you board the subway cars.

George walks over to one side of the stage where he waits alone, away from the rest of the crowd.

Sam paused the video, "here is George." He then points to the screen and moves his finger over to someone in the other crowd of people. "This is the third victim; he is standing here at the edge of this cluster of people here."

Sam pressed play. The third victim looks over and notices George. He then walks those hundred feet or so and places his hand on George's shoulder. George jumped a bit as if he had awakened him from a deep sleep. George turned and faced him with his box of stuff in-between them. There appeared to be two or three seconds of conversation between the two. George then turned his back to the man and appeared to head in the opposite direction of the third victim. George made one step forward, not even shifting his weight off of

his planted foot and from behind him, the man,

which he had just turned away from, was flung

about one hundred and fifty feet away at an

extremely fast speed. It looked as if he had jumped

the impossible distance. You could almost hear a

thud on that soundless tape as he hit the tile wall.

When he fell off the wall and onto the track, you

could see the tile shattered and began to break off.

It almost seemed to defy gravity the way he was

propelled sideways at such a fast speed. By this

time, everyone on the tracks was facing the man

and George. About two or three seconds went past

with the man just waving his hand from the tracks

but laying on his back on the tracks. He looked as if

he was badly injured he could not move. People

from the crowd started to run over to where he

laid. Before anyone could get those hundred feet or so the train struck him. The train looked as if it flew past the people on the platform going ninety miles an hour or more.

"Wow." Dr. Williams watched the last little bit of the tape where George did not even look back at the man and just kept walking out of the frame. "Wow again," she said as Sam stopped the video. "I don't know what to say to this. He didn't do it. George was right. If that man was flung out on those tracks that fast by George, who never took his hands of that box of crap, then George sprouted two more arms in his back to do it.

Sam cuts in, "There was no one else around the two of them at the time. What do you think could cause a man weighing about two hundred pounds to be propelled out onto the tracks like that? I can't figure it out. We have all watched this many times and can't even see in slow motion any expression change on the man. It was like he froze and was flung out on the tracks like a weightless rag doll." He puts down the remote.

John, the Assistant District Attorney, hops into the conversation, when Sam paused for breath. "I can't charge him for this crime with this tape if he admits to it we can suppress the tape to prosecute him." He was wearing a very fine tailored suit, and readjusted his weight on the tabletop as he said this to Dr. Williams.

"You are one piece of work. What in hell makes you think I'm going to allow something like that happen? You saw that video there was nothing he did wrong. He turned his back to the man and was walking away. He did not push him. In fact, he never laid a hand on the man. He put his hand on George's shoulder. I will give the judge a call myself if I have just to keep this tape in evidence. Now if you gentlemen don't mind I have to go piss. Then I'm going back in there to get the rest of this out of the way. No one is to go in there." Dr. Williams turned and under her breath calls them all "Dirtbags."

After the battle with the ADA, she walked back down the hall with the sound of her stilettos making a clacking sound on the old marble floor. She paused right outside the interrogation room door and began to relive the events in the video and think about how she would bring this up in conversation. After her prolonged pause, she opened the door and walked in.

The Interview

"Well, George I have some news to share with you." Her stilettos made the same clacking noise on the way from the door to the table. She looked at the mirror and said "Can one of you fine gentlemen bring us some more coffee please." She finished the short walk to the table and took her seat.

"Dr. Williams, you are forgetting something." He said

"What is that George?"

Just then before you were going to walk out of the room you had something you were going to ask me. I think it was going to be important." It seemed as if George knew exactly what this question was going to be and to bait her to ask it.

"George I can't remember off the top of my head so much has happened in the last couple of minutes." Just as she finished her sentence, she looked down at her pad where she had been making her notes and noticed in large bold letters **PARENTS DEATH** written on the pad. "Oh yeah, I remember the question and what we were talking about before I walked out."

"What happened to your mom and dad? You said that they were killed."

"Yep, they were."

Chapter 11

Mom and Dad

"I guess I need to give you just a little history here about my family before I get into all about the death." Dr. Williams drew a line on her notepad to indicate that she was starting a new subject again. She wrote under the line Mom and Dad.

"My family came from old money. The oil industry was good to my great grandparents in the late 1800's. My great-grandfather was a self-educated businessman. He didn't go to any fancy Ivy League school. In fact, he only had an eighth-grade education. He just had some common knowledge of the universe. He read a lot and soon noticed a trend in the companies opening. Although the automobile industry was just a dream at the time, my great-grandfather knew what to do. He took his life savings, and as big a loan from the bank to start an oil company. He purchased many acres of land in the Midwest.

After many years of hard work, he struck oil on the land. Once automobiles were being mass-produced he opened a refinery. My family during this period amassed a large fortune. He became so comfortable he purchased a couple hundred acres in New England. My great grandfather, being of new money, wanted to make a statement. He had built an enormous house he called Jasmine Hills after the fresh jasmine grown on the property.

Jasmine Hills was so large it was even equipped with its own chapel. The outer stone was grey the roof was charcoal lack. There was a library of solid maple that spanned three floors. Most of the walls were hardwood judges paneling. On the grounds, there were also several barns with prizewinning stallions. I still remember my grandmother telling me that some of the horses were worth hundreds of thousands of dollars. My favorite horse was the Clydesdale named Billy Boy. This was truly a beautiful place.

Shortly after the house was completed there was an offer for my great-grandfather to get out of the oil business. A man by the name of Rockefeller wanted him to sell. My great-grandfather at first did not want to. After many turndowns the railway company that Rockefeller controlled raised the prices more than triple for shipping to and from the refinery my great-grandfather conceded and retired.

Soon after my great-grandfather sold out he died and left my father's father in charge. The deal with Standard Oil continued to pay out because of the stock acquired during the purchase. My

grandfather was an only child like my father, and I

was. My grandfather differed greatly from my

great-grandfather being educated at Cambridge. He

came back to the states shortly after that to finish

an advanced business degree from Harvard

Business School. When he took over the household

and the family money, he put it to work in the New

York Stock Exchange.

By the time, my father stepped to the plate.

I was very young. He had also been to Harvard and

one summer abroad. He did that stint at the

University in Paris studying architecture. What my

father found fascinating in Paris was that on

weekends he could travel to a little principality

named Monaco. The thing that drew him here on

the weekends was not the beauty of the city or the

ocean view. It was the Casino Monte Carlo. He loved to gamble and drink. He was so addicted to this he could not stop dreaming about all the bright lights and brilliant noises."

Angelica cleared her throat and said, "He had a personality hedged toward addiction?"

"Yes he did very much so. I was about four when he became head of the family. By the time, he died I was eighteen and had just graduated from High school, and the family was broke. That's why I live in a little apartment."

"So the gambling caused him to go broke? That is a lot of money just to piss away don't you think?"

"You have no Idea. This man could not stop once he started. In the high-roller section in an illegal casino, he became addicted to cocaine. This was just the beginning of his downfall."

Just as George was finishing up his sentence Sam walked into the room. In one hand he had a pot of coffee, and in the other there were a couple packets of cream and sugar. "I didn't remember how you guys take your coffee, so I brought a couple of these packets for you." As he placed them on the table, Sam glanced over at George and gave him an angry look. "Enjoy..."

After Sam had left the room, George had this full body shiver. Out of all the people he had met in the police station Sam was the only one that made George really uncomfortable. Dr. Williams noticed the uncomfortable look between the two and decided to take a moment to put George at ease again. This was not the only time she had noticed him becoming increasingly uneasy.

"Why do you let him do that to you? You know that he is just doing that because he knows it makes you uncomfortable. He wants you to crack under pressure. He is a cop that's what they do. I'm a Psychologist. I have the philosophy that you will not tell me anything unless you are as comfortable with the situation as possible. So sit back, relax, and take a deep breath. Once you are back in a good calm good continue telling me about your father. You had just got to the part where he had become addicted to cocaine at an underground gambling establishment."

George gathered his composure and poured himself some coffee using his loosely handcuffed hands. "Well, I think I'm going to be fine. He just gives me the creeps. He reminds me with those looks he gives me, of that grave digger from Oak Hill Cemetery."

"Humm." Dr. Williams noted this little piece of information down in her notepad. "I think he *is* a grave digger," she said under her breath with a chuckle. From behind the glass Sam frowned.

"Well, back to my father." George picked up his coffee cup and took a sip with a loud slurping noise. "He could never be happy with anything. Sometimes he would win at the gambling establishments. But most of the time he would loose and loose big. He sometimes would go into debt with the loan sharks by hundreds of thousands of dollars.

My mother never knew what was going on. She was an extremely kept woman. As long as she had a new designer dress and a couple of new pieces of jewelry every year she didn't care what my father did. He would come home most of the time, toward the end of their life, drunk and strung out on drugs. She wouldn't let him into the master wing of the house. She always made him sleep in the guest quarters.

One time when, I was in high school, my mother threw a large dinner party for the aristocracy of the country." Pausing, looking at the good doctor with great pride. "My mother's parties were to die for. There were many famous people that come to join us from Hollywood to British Royalty. The house my great-grandfather had built was great for such events. There were enough guest suites to house one hundred and fifteen guests. After all this was the largest house in America.

Right as the live orchestra had begun to play, and the pre-dinner cocktails were being served, my father came home. He was wearing his tuxedo ripped to shreds. He stumbled into the great hall of the house and collapsed onto the marble entryway in front of the orchestra. The butlers dropped what they were doing to pick him up and brought him to the master wing of the house.

My mother was obviously embarrassed and excused herself to go find out exactly what had happened. Once into the master suite, me behind her, she slapped his already bloody face. 'What the hell is wrong with you?' She said 'You were supposed to be here hours ago.' My father just mumbled something unrecognizable. My mother and I left him there to sober up and burnoff the

booze and whatever else he had in his system.

Once in the hallway with the servants, my

mother excused them to finish serving drinks and

prepare the dining room. My mother surprised me

at how strong she was during this time. I expected

her to breakdown crying from embarrassment, but

instead she straitened herself up and told me to

wait outside the door. She went in and about two

minutes later she came out all freshened up, with

new white gloves on replacing her bloodied ones,

and ready to return to the party.

We went through the rest of the party

without incident. After lunch the next day when all

of the guests had left, my mother called a family

meeting in the grand library. She asked my father

to explain what had happened. My father and I sat

The Interview

on the opposite sofa, and my mother paced on the rug between them. He told us that he had been playing a game of cards and lost some money. Once he was busted, he got credit from the house and lost all of that money. He had never borrowed money from this man before and did not completely understand his terms. He did drugs and drank a lot while he played with this man's money. Before he decided to call for his car, the loan shark wanted payment in full plus fees. My father told us that he had forgotten his checkbook because before he had left, he had changed into his tuxedo to be ready for the party.

He explained to us that the debt was only twenty thousand with another two thousand in fees. This amount was ok with my mother because the party had cost three times that, so as you can understand she didn't even bat an eye at the amount. 'Go on,' she kept telling him. He said that they let the valet call for his car and the shark's goons punched him in the face and the stomach and threw him in the trunk of his Bentley. They took him to a warehouse in the center of town and beat him to a bloody pulp, and kept the car making him sign it over to them. They then put him in the trunk of another car and dumped him out at the gate of the property.

My mother was not convinced of the story. She dismissed him and said that she would get him some help to deal with his addictions. He agreed to undergo treatment. Later that afternoon she booked him a flight to the Betty Ford clinic, which was new at the time, to start his treatment. She instructed him to check himself in and undergo treatment for two weeks. If at that time she felt comfortable with him coming home, she would allow it."

"Wow, George your mother seemed like a strong woman."

George straightened up and presented nearly perfect posture. "See I never thought my mother was that strong until the party. She had to be. I always thought my mother to be someone that expected greatness, but never someone with the strength to handle someone of my father's caliber."

Sounding like a feminist, Dr. Williams added, "I think it's wonderful that you have this memory of power about your mother."

"Yeah, I never really thought about it until now but you are right. My mother does deserve credit for her strength." George kept his posture perfect while discussing his mother. It was obvious that he was proud.

"How did you feel about your father at this point?"

"I hated him. I thought he was scum. He never was around that much when I was a child and never treated my mother with much respect. I was angry with him. In some small way, I thought that he could possibly redeem himself with this Betty Ford thing."

I kind of felt relieved when my father left a couple days later. I knew that I would be leaving for college at the end of the summer, and wanted to leave my mother in a good place. Knowing that my father was going to seek help for his problem made me feel more comfortable with the whole going away thing. Little did I know at that time that my father would continue to be a disappointment for my mother and Me.

I found out shortly after my father had left for the Ford Clinic, the exact scope of his addiction. He had changed his fight plans to Vegas when he arrived at the airport. We actually didn't find out until it was too late. My father in one week's time had gone through all of the family's money in Vegas. When my mother got a call from him saying that he was coming home and that he felt much better. He told her that he would be coming in on the redeye flight not to wait up he would talk to her the next morning.

Early that morning I went out to go shopping for a new computer to go off to college with. At the time, a computer was the size of a small closet. My father had come home during the night like he had told my mother. When I left, the luggage was still in the parlor. I went out and did my shopping for about three hours and returned home.

When I was coming into the driveway, there were three strange black Cadillac sedans speeding away from the house. I come up to the house to find a van being packed up outside the front entrance to the house. It looked as if they were throwing five-gallon fuel cans into the back of the van. As I pulled my car in behind them, I noticed they were not employed as part of the household.

I put the car into park and turned off the engine. A man dressed all in black waved at me. I felt really nervous about this strange guy with a cratered and scared face. The wave he gave me was like a hail you would give a cab. I stepped out of my

The Interview

Saab, and he shouted at me, 'Your parents have been waiting on you.'

From the passenger side of the van, someone else stepped out. This man was tall and fat. He looked like someone who had retired from boxing years ago, and had developed a large gut from no exercise. He walked over next to the man loading the rear of the van. I stayed next to my car.

The fat man never said a word, but I asked, 'Where are my parents.' The scarface man said, 'Inside.'

I said 'Would you guys show me?' Then as if it were a natural reaction to such a question scarface pulled a handgun from his back and said, 'Sure.' I immediately stopped. The big fat man walked over to me.

Christopher McDonald

Scarface said, 'Follow me and don't try anything funny or Big Joe here will snap you like a twig before I shoot you.' The thugs lead me into the house where we walked down the hall heading to the Grand Library. As we walked down the hall, I noticed there were many colorful balloons stapled to the ceiling by the tied end. All of them were filled with a liquid about two inches or so the rest was filled with air. As I walked down the corridors of Jasmine Hill, I could smell the sickening smell of gasoline. I realized then that the liquid in the balloons were gas.

As we reached the lower floor entrance to the library, I realized there was something wrong. I noticed next to the fireplace that there were two people sitting back to back in some old Queen Ann style chairs in the library. I quickly come to the realization that the two people were my parents. The thugs had tied them to the chairs. As I processed what I was seeing I noticed every detail about them in slow motion, it seemed. Big Joe Was pushing me in holding my hands behind my back as my body went limp like a spaghetti noodle. He had to pull me up and push me over to where my parent's lifeless bodies were. Scarface pulled another Queen Ann chair from one of the study tables and placed it about twenty feet away from my parent's.

Scarface yelled 'Sitdown you maggot.' Big Joe had to place me in the chair. I was still in shock and trying to absorb all that was going on. As I was placed in the chair, I could hear a crackling sound that the old dry wood in the chair made. Once in the chair scarface duct taped my hands behind my back and my waist to the chair. I was stuck.

I then came to the understanding of how my parents meet their demise. They had been suffocated. There were clear plastic bags around their heads and duct taped to their necks. I could do nothing at this point but wonder if I would meet the same fate as my parents. After all, I had been duct taped to the chair in the same fashion as them and a member of the same family. I asked them both over and over again, 'What did we do? What do you want?' Scarface said, lying of course, 'we don't know. All we know is we were hired to do a job that no one else wanted to do. So here we are doing it. You get to watch the house you grew up in, burn along with your parents.'

The Interview

The smell of gas flowed through the whole house. You could almost get high off of the fumes. As I sat there staring at my parents, tears streaming down my face, I could not speak.

'Go get the rest of the gas,' Scarface demanded from the big guy. Without saying a word as usual, he just went on outside.

I asked them what the hell they wanted from me. I even went as far as groveling to the Scarface man. I pleaded and said that I would give him any amount of money he wanted to spare my life. 'You don't have any money to give me,' was the response.

I couldn't believe that. I said very forcefully to Scarface, Do you even see the house you are burning down? We have money.

That's when he informed me of the reality behind the situation. He had been hired because my father had skipped out on debt in Vegas. There was nothing in the bank accounts or with the Wall Street firms. All that was left was this house. He informed me that the people that hired him didn't want to wait for such a large piece of property to sell. He wanted to send a message. The message was that you didn't borrow the money if you can't pay it back.

So you see Dr. Williams this was a major turning point in my life. I was faced with the reality that my parents were dead and that I was flat broke."

"I see." Dr. Williams said. "Do you know who hired the two men to do the job?"

The Interview

"No, but I have always wondered if the people leaving in the black cars were the people or person who ordered the hit on my parents. I have my suspicions though. It sounds like one of those mob stories to me. It reminded me of that movie *The Godfather.* In that movie when someone who owed them money and didn't have a way to pay someone got 'whacked.'

"Do you really think that they would do such a thing like this? Dr. Williams replied.

"Well, talking to the feds leads me to believe that nothing was going to be done about this. I had no ally or hope of restitution. "

"Do you need a moment or can you finish telling me what happened to you in the library and how you got out of the house?" Dr. Williams was vigorously writing notes on her pad.

George began to top off his coffee and cleared his throat. "Dr. Williams there is not one day in my life that I don't think back on what happened that day. I'm 28 years old, and this is still as fresh as yesterday. There isn't a detail that I haven't run over and again in my mind.

I can still smell the gas all these years later. Remember the position of my mother head gazing over at me from in front of a large fireplace. The cracking of the wood as the large companion poured his barrel of fuel along the bottoms of the bookcases. No detail has escaped me Dr. Williams."

"Ok then go on and finish I won't interrupt again." She still ever so vigorously notes the conversation.

"Your fine asking anything you need to. I just get a little emotional about this." George pours

The Interview

himself some more coffee from the carafe. "I find that looking back on this time in my life will help me understand the future better. I need to finish this before I get too absorbed in it.

After the two men had tied me to a chair, I continued to cry out to please spare me and let me live. I pleaded with them that I would never tell a single person that I had seen them. You know the usual survival instincts that a person possesses. They just mocked me and continued to pour on the accelerants. After I come to the conclusion that my pleas were not going to be granted, I began to formulate a plan to escape.

While they were looting the place for silver and gold plated items, I was looking at my exit options. There were the windows behind me leading to the front yard. There was the option of the stairs leading up. The thought then came to me that fire moves up, and I moved on. The only other option was out the way they had brought me in. Through the hall where they had placed all of the colorful balloons filled with gasoline.

I have to think quickly I heard them move metal objects back out to the van. I then heard the wood crack in the hall as they started back down toward the library. The big guy is saying nothing looked at me as he walked over to my mother. I began to struggle as if I were going to be able to break the duct tape wrapped around my waist. He grabbed her necklace... I began to struggle even more powerfully. 'Leave her alone,' I yelled as I tried to free myself. Knocking my chair over crashing into the hardwood floors, I watched as he ripped the ornate jewel from my mother's neck. He walked out of the room as I yelled out in utter disgust.

I heard the two talking from outside and couldn't makeout a word of it, and then I heard the door of the van shut and the engine crank. They drove down the driveway. Almost simultaneously, I began to hear the wood creek again as if there was someone walking down the hall coming toward the library. Only this creaking was faster and louder as if it were an elephant this time. There was no beast trampling down the hall; it was the FIRE.

Almost as if it were instinct I jumped up with the chair still strapped to my back. The adrenalin pumping through my body I backed the chair into the nearest hard object, a bookcase. The fire began to spread around the room from the hall.

Christopher McDonald

I quickly realized that the hall was not going to be my exit point.

The chair creaked and cracked as I slammed it into a bookcase. It finally broke free leaving me more mobile to run for the Tiffany stained glass windows. I picked up a bust of Shakespeare and tossed it through the window and hurled myself through after it as the fire had finally reached me. When I had slammed myself into the bookcase to break the chair, I got some of the fuel on me that was used to soak the bookcase. As soon as I was outside, and the first major explosion hit I found myself knocked to the grass and on fire. I rolled, to extinguish the fire, to barely move far enough to escape the next large blast from the house.

I sat out on the front lawn of the house a safe distance away. My home was crumbling. It had taken a half hour before fire trucks came. There was no saving anything. It just had to burn to a pile of smoldering coals.

The police took me to the hospital for treatment of my burns and cuts. I went to a private room with a guard posted outside, and my arm handcuffed to the bed. I found myself suddenly having to answer questions to rule myself out as a suspect. It wasn't long before my story checked out, and I was able to move freely. I was given a protective detail until I went off to college. The college that accepted me, Yale, gave me a full ride including room and board. I suppose they took pity on me after hearing my circumstances; I mean I would have. Wouldn't you?"

After a short pause, "Yes I do believe I would. You just went through something very traumatic. Did anyone ever try to contact you about, you know, *finishing the job?*"

"No never. To this day I live a pretty low-key existence. Could we get some more coffee? I think I'm running low."

"Yes George we will get more." Dr. Williams looked at the mirror and held the carafe up as if to demand it to be full again. "I just have a couple other things I want to ask you on the subject before we move on.

How did things at Yale go after all of this happened?

George cleared his throat once again. "Well, as you can imagine, after something like this, I began to see someone about my sleepless nights and my anxiety. I avoided circumstances where I had to be in front of people. I barely made it through speech class. All four years there are just a blur to me."

Doctor Williams pushed her chair away from the table. "Well, George I think I have enough information to go on. I will see you tomorrow at the courthouse before we see the judge. I think you are innocent George. I saw the video and will give a full account in court."

George sighed. "I honestly don't think that will help me much."

"George don't worry," was the reply.

George just looked back down at his hands and pondered his future. "I won't." He said.

Doctor Williams assured him that she would have everything in order by the next day and would not let anything happen to him. Your attorney and I will meet with you before the hearing tomorrow." On this note, she packed up her things and left. George just nodded not lifting his head from the table as she left the room.

Chapter 12

Long Night

After Dr. Williams had left, George was, of course, subjected to the same treatment as before. The officers verbally abused him as he was handcuffed and led downstairs to get his ice shower. Once in his cell, this time cell A not C; he was able to relax and contemplate the events of the day. Like most people in a troubling situation, you never need excessive time to think about your problems.

Once in the cell George began to pace back and forth in his cell going over what might happen in court the next day. George never had been to court. He had never even gotten as much as a traffic ticket. He began to analyze what was going on. One by one he went through the events of the day trying to determine whether or not he even could have killed those people and how.

The Interview

Talking to himself, he began to arrange things in his mind. 'Whitney was mad at me. This much is clear. I could have been my usual awkward self and said something insulting to her on our date. I can't be sure what I did exactly. Whatever it was she was pissed the next day at work. Maybe I should have given her time to cool down.' The entire time George is running down the details he is pacing back and forth trying to calm himself.

'What about the lunch? What happened there? We were talking that's all. Why did she want to get away from me? She must have still been mad about before. Why though? She had plenty of time to cool down. All I needed was a chance to apologize.' George paused for a while. He went over in his mind the events that happened next. The thing with the bus, He saw the bus. She didn't.

Why? Why did she just stop, when I yelled out to her? She didn't even look at the bus.' This was strange to George looking back on it now. Why did she just pause when he yelled out to her? 'Was it the fact that I yelled STOP? Who takes that sort of thing literally? Who would just stop dead in their tracks and go nowhere.' Never the less Whitney was dead, and he had other things to consider. His boss

'When Whitney was hit by a bus, I must have been in shock. That would explain the situation in the elevator. That must be why it seemed to be as if I had to push my way out. I must have been imagining this. That is probably why I don't remember much about my boss. I just remember going in his office and exiting. I'm not too sure how to account for the loss of time there.'

George continued to pace.

A guard approached the cell. As he come, closer George could read the embroidered name patch over his left shirt pocket. "Mathis," he said as he approached.

"Whats wrong?" Mathis asked.

"Nothing. Why?" George said.

"I can hear you mumbling all the way at the end of the hall. Are you having a nervous breakdown?" The officer asked.

"No, I'm just talking to myself. I do that when I am nervous. Please ignore me. I just was working out what was going on with me. Surely everyone is guilty of talking to himself once in a while."

"I guess we are." The officer replied. "If you need anything just yell. I am Officer Mathis." George replied, "Thank you. I will try to keep it down I just need to process things. By the way if you don't mind me saying, you are much kinder than any of the other officers I have encountered over the last couple days. How long have you been doing this?"

After a slight chuckle the chubby twenty-something replied, "This is my first night. I have been told you are dangerous and psychotic. For me to stay clear."

"I see." George replied as Mathis turned to walk back to the guard station. George noticed as he walked away that he didn't have a proper badge on his chest it was an embroidered one under his name. That must mean he is in training or not out of the academy yet.

When Mathis returned to the end of the hall, he sat down, and picked up an iPad, swiped and started tapping away. George sat and wondered if he was playing a game or surfing the web or just a really fast reader of eBooks. After collecting his thoughts, he had a seat on the cot.

'How did it happen?' he said to himself. 'The elevator back in the building. I must have been in shock. Or just imagined the people there.' George put his hands up to his face and closed his eyes. 'I'm going crazy.'

'When I got back to our floor I had to go see the boss.' George stood again and began to pace. 'Did I sitdown? Why can't I remember the details?' The cloud fogging his memory was not lifting. 'I remember the secretary and telling her that he was busy. Why can't I remember? I do recall the jest of the conversation. I know he did fire me. Why can't I remember? What went on in the office? That's what scares me.' George paused and tried extra hard to remember but no luck.

'What was the next thing I remember? Gee. I don't recall much more until the police car and here. The subway seems to be just a flash in my memory. This is frustrating.'
George yelled. "Officer Mathis. Could you comedown here, please? I have a favor to ask you."

Mathis putdown his iPad and gave it a long thought. He stood and shifted his weight from foot to foot as if he wasn't sure he wanted to know what the favor was. George was holding the bars of his holding cell saying, 'Please,' under his breath. As if

The Interview

Mathis had some change of heart or just wanted to know what the request was he complied and walked to the holding cell where George was anxiously waiting.

"Thank you so much." George started. "I need to see the video of the subway."

"What are you talking about?" Mathis looked puzzled by the strange request. "What video of the subway?"

"My Psychologist went to view a video of me in the subway. I need to see it. It is on the other side of the mirror in the interrogation room."

"Dude even if I knew where the video was I doubt I would have the access to that. I don't know where in the building interrogation rooms are."

"I do," George said.

"No… No. I see what you are doing here. I am not letting you out of here." Mathis turned to walk back to his iPad game.

"Stop please," George yelled out. Mathis kept walking. In one last plea George shouted, "PLEASE." As he shouted, Mathis stopped and noticed the lights dim then brighten back up quickly. He turned and walked back to the cell.

George did it. He influenced the officer. "I need you to let me out of here. I promise I will return after we view the video. I will even let you handcuff me."

Mathis said, "George listen… I will shoot you if you try anything funny." Mathis patted his side like he had a sidearm. He was in training and had only been to the range once. He barely knew how to load his gun. Much less shoot it.

The Interview

"Mathis Please!" George said.

"Even If I knew where the film was what do you expect to accomplish here?" Mathis said.

"I know it's a long shot but I do know that I did not push anybody in front of a bus or train or a speeding car. I could not have done this."

Mathis shook his head in agreement and went with his gut. "I need you to face the back of the cell and put your hands behind you back."

George did as he was asked and said "Thank you."

"Don't thank me yet we haven't even started." Mathis stepped into the cell and placed the cuffs on George. He checked for the tightness and determined that they were as tight as they would be.

"OK," George said. "I think the video is on the second floor. We just need to go up there and check it out."

"Wait..." Mathis said. "This has to go my way. I need to make sure we are alone. Wait here, and I will see if we can even make it to where you need to be." Mathis climbed the staircase next to the emergency exit. He looked out the window on the first floor and noticed no one was there except the night watchman. All he was doing was watching *I Love Lucy* reruns.

Mathis proceeded to climb the stairs and look out the second-floor hallway. As he suspected, no one was there, so he stormed back to the basement to get his prisoner.

"What did you see?" George asked.

The Interview

"Nothing." Mathis Said, "Come on let's get this over with." He waved at George and as he instructed followed him to the stairs. They climbed the staircase and avoided the sitcom watching guard on the ground floor to get to the second floor where the tape was held.

George said as they exited the stairwell. "I know where we are. The room is just over there." They both took off running toward the room where George's tape was. As they reached the door, they heard the elevator bell ding indicating someone was on their floor. The door to the room, of course, was locked. Mathis at this point knew his career was over in law enforcement.

George touched the door handle with his bound hands and the door unlocked with a click. "I knew we would be ok," he said to Mathis.

Christopher McDonald

They both ducked inside the room as the *I Love Lucy* guy stepped off the elevator. Mathis put his index finger to George's lips like he was protecting him. The Guard walked to the end of the hall and went back to the elevator door. He walked in and went on his rounds upward.

"Ok." Mathis Said. "You are here. I guess that the tape of the subway over there. He pointed to the TV set with the recorder setup.

"Thank you so much Mathis. I can't even tell you how much this means to me. I need to clear my name." George went to the TV set and pushed in the tape in. After the snow cleared he witnessed the truth. He saw that he never touched the person on the subway. He saw that when he shouted at the guy (A former associate) that he was flung by some force other than him onto the tracks.

The Interview

"Mathis do you know what this means?" George turned to the officer.

Mathis was not there.

Alarms sounded, and police began to scramble. George was found on the second floor of the police percent with his hand bound in cuffs behind his back. He was mumbling something about his companion Mathis. Of course, the officers knew no one by that name and escorted George back to his cell.

The official report would state that the murder suspect escaped his cell and went rogue on a spree through the precinct. The report went on to say that he was babbling something about the subway killings. No one knew how to interpret this. Maybe Dr. Williams could when she returned tomorrow.

260

After a call to the captain of the precinct was phoned about the incident George was moved to the county lockup.

Chapter 13

Research

Dr. Williams reached her house on an uneasy wind. She knew something was off about what she was doing and knew she had to do something about it. She entered the foyer and placed her briefcase in the floor. She went straight to her study (A glorified library). From the wet bar, she poured a generous glass of merlot and took a seat behind her cherry wood desk.

'What in the world could explain what was happening to this man?' she asked herself. 'What could explain the things that happened?'
She sipped a glass of wine while she thought. She opened her Apple laptop and turned to the most conventional thing on the planet, Google.

'I know there is no such thing as paranormal. What do I type? It was obvious that he didn't push the guy on to the tracks. I have actual proof of this. What to type?' She let her fingers do the walking, and typed *paranormal.*

Of course, one of the top pages she came to was that of Wikipedia. It told her what she already knew. She knew that there was no scientific explanation for what had happened. She continued on down the list. Then she came across some research being done in mind control and telekinesis.

Surprisingly The Catholic Church was actually doing the mind control research. A group of priest in Switzerland has been doing research on pheromones. They had discovered a group of chemicals that can potentially control a person's dopamine pathways. In some studies, she noticed that people would become catatonic for some time.

In this study, the clergy was testing plant pheromones.

This whole train of thought gave Dr. Williams an idea. She began to research the term Psychokinetic. With every click of the mouse, she dove deeper and deeper into the world of the supernatural. She soon left conventional science behind. At 2:37 am there was a breakthrough. She picked up the phone and called John. John answered in an expectantly sleepy voice. "Dr. Williams?"

"John, I need you to find me a Dr. S. King with North Carolina State University."

"Dr. Williams its 2:30 in the morning. This couldn't wait? John asked."

The Interview

"NO. Get your ass up and find out how to get in touch with him. He has been researching pheromone mind control."

"Dr. Williams there is no such......"
She interrupts, "John if you want to keep your job shut up and find him. He is the key for this whole thing to make any sense."

"Ok ok... I will see you at the courthouse in the morning with the information. Try to get some sleep."

"You just worry about finding Dr. King."
After she had hung up the phone, she continued to read. She found information on how primal animals could use their pheromones to control another animal. 'How the hell can you prove any of this in court?'

She putdown her glass of wine and went back to the wet bar. 'I need something stronger than this shit.' She opened up a bottle of scotch and poured a nice tall glass.

'What will I tell the judge? And what will I have to back it up? The tape is not going to be enough, I know." She sat and stared at the screen intently. "I have been to enough of these things to know that no matter what, the judge will just want to know the basics. He will just want me to tell him whether or not he is capable of standing trial and my professional opinion on the defendant. I have to be clever enough to lead him into asking me about the crimes."

Dr. Williams began to pour over every bit of verifiable information on the subject she could get her hands on. She knew she needed to get Dr. King

The Interview

in touch with George's lawyer first thing in the morning so that they may be able to put together a plausible defense.

She looked up after what had been a couple of minutes to her had actually been hours. It was 6am, and she had to be at the courthouse by 8:30 the hearing was at 9am.

She jumped up from her desk, "Shit," she yelled. She ran upstairs where she was hoping to beat her husband to the bathroom so she could get ready. As she topped the stairs, she heard the water running. 'Damn, he's up.' She was hoping to not have to explain anything to him so she could get ready and not break her train of thought. She went to the closet to find her most professional pants suit to wear to court. She grabbed a pair Jimmy Choo's to match. She heard he shower cut off.

"Babe?" She heard her husband's voice.

"I'm in the closet getting my clothes together." She said

"Tell me you didn't sleep in your office again."

"No babe, I was downstairs in the study reading and must have dozed off." Of course, this was a lie she had not been to sleep and drank a quarter bottle of scotch while doing it.

She looked up to see her husband standing in the doorway between the closet and the bathroom fully nude and half erect. "You know hun, we can get some alone time in before I have to leave. I can always grab another shower with you."

"Babe I would love to, but I have to be in court." She shrugged trying not to look at how great he looked standing in the doorway now fully erect.

The Interview

"I'm sorry." She stepped past him and began to undress in front of the shower door.

"Ok. You better be at home this evening; you owe me double." He said smirking at her.

She turned and looked over her shoulder just before stepping in the shower. "It's a date." She went on in and cut the water on. She began thinking of how she could lead the line of questioning in the courtroom to bring in her opinion of the paranormal.

Chapter 14

County

Upon arrival at the County Jail, a Sheriff's deputy met the city police officer at intake. He handed him a file about the upcoming court appearance that morning and a briefing of his charges.

"I'll take it from here sir." The tall slender bald deputy said.

"Watch yourself with this one." The officer warned. "He tried to escape tonight."

"He won't get out of here I can assure you sir. Thanks for the warning though it will be duly noted." The Intake deputy raised his hand in a dismissive manner. To this the city officer hopped in his car and drove off.

Once inside George was asked to sit on a bench. He looked around the room. On the opposite bench was a woman beat to hell with her hands cuffed behind her back. She looked at him and said. "What are you in for honey?"

George replied, "A big misunderstanding."

She looked back up at him trying to squint her recently bruised black eye and said. "That's what we are all in here for, one big misunderstanding. They don't see it the way we do. To us it's a misunderstanding to them its a crime." She laughed and went back to trying to sleep with her back to the cement wall.

George was greeted by a large man in a military green outfit telling him to stand. He must have been ex-army or something because he kept the hair GI cut. George did as he said. He said, "This way please," lifting his right arm pointing to a room.

George looked and did as he said and walked into the room. As he walked in he noticed that the room was some sort of shower and assumed that he was about to get yet another cold shower. This time the deputy stepped in with him, and the door clanked shut behind him. The deputy was wearing rubber exam gloves.

"Take everything off, even your underwear. He stood at the doorway with his arms crossed and waited. At first George did nothing. He gave that nod with his head likes, 'go ahead or I will for you.'

George began to disrobe by taking off his shirt. Then off went his pants, shoes, and socks.

"I said everything." Pointing at is boxers and undershirt. George reluctantly complied and took them off with a look of embarrassment on his face.

The Interview

The officer who has obviously done this task thousands of time in his career watched with no shame. He told George to bend at the knees and spread his legs out in a squatting position. George did as he asked and soon found himself in close proximity to the deputy. He began to search George from head to toe for contraband.

After the degrading act was complete George was told to put his clothes in a bag he took from his pocket. George did as he asked with no reluctance. He was then told to wait here a minute while he retrieved him some clothes. George was left alone for what felt like an eternity before he returned with an orange jumpsuit, socks, and plastic slippers.

"Follow me. The deputy commanded. George, of course, did as he asked and was lead into a large open holding room with many other people in orange suits. "Sit in one of the blue chairs and wait on your name to be called for processing."

After sitting he noticed the room was divided in half with blue and pink chairs and women, were in the pink chairs. It looked as if he were in a room with a bunch of drunks and prostitutes.

He sat in one of the blue chairs on the first row. After nodding off, a sheriff deputy called him over to the desk. The deputy asked George to stand on the blue line taped to the floor and look at a dot on the wall. After a flash, his mug shot was recorded and printed on a bracelet with his prisoner ID on it.

"Stand outside that door." The deputy pointed at a large steel door with no window or handle.

The door opened, and George was asked to step through by another deputy. This whole

The Interview

experience made him think that this is what cattle felt like being led to slaughter. Once through the door George was instructed to pick up a blanket and a mattress for his bunk. And lead to the door to a massive two-story cellblock.

"You will be in number 30 on the second floor." The deputy told him.

George stepped in. With a loud clank that startled him to his core the door slammed behind him.

Everyone in the block turned to look at the newbie that just walked through the door. George took a survey of the room. There were obvious cliques. Some men were at a table in the center of the block playing a game of cards. There was one man off by himself reading an Iris Johansen novel. There was a group of Latino men leaned against a rail looking down at him. There was another group of thug looking men making what looked like a tattoo on the back of another inmate.

George took a deep breath and began to walk to the stairs. He was thinking to himself the whole time that he couldn't do this. The eyes of the other men in the room just followed him as he made it to the stairs. After he had reached the top, the Latino group said something to one another about him. George obviously didn't know what they said. He just nodded and went on. As he passed other open cells, he looked in to find more men doing pushups and other exercises in their cells.

Once in number 30 George took a deep breath. He notices someone had a mattress and blanket on the bottom bunk of number 30 so he knew instantly that he had to take the top. He placed the rolled up cot on the top bunk and made a makeshift bed. He noticed then that there would be no pillows. Instead of pillows there was a hump at one end of the cot that would serve as a pillow.

Thinking to himself, 'the whole pillow thing must have been enacted for a reason. Someone must have smothered someone with one.'

George finished making up his bed to notice what time it actually was. It was 6:30 in the morning and everyone had just got up for the day. 'Where did the time go he wondered?'

George walked out of his cell to notice everyone stopped and looked at him. He could not help but feel uneasy about this. Seeing as how everyone in the room had probably been convicted of horrible things. Hopefully, Dr. Williams would be able to help him clear his name today and free himself from all this mess.

'I wonder if the state will issue a formal apology after this is all over? They would have to do something I would think. I could sue them if they don't... No... That's not the type of person I am.' The group of Latinos was watching George as he mumbled to himself. When George looked up to see that they had noticed, he went back into his cell hopped up on the top bunk. He buried himself in the corner with his knees tucked to his chest.

The guys that had noticed him mumbling decided to go checkout this new inmate. The three Latinos walked the short distance to cell 30 talking in their own dialect about George no less.

The obvious leader of the group told the other two to wait outside the cell while he went in. The

The Interview

man was about six five and two hundred and fifty pounds, at least twice George's size. He wore his orange jumpsuit as pants with the sleeves wrapped around his waist exposing his tattooed chest.

As he walked in the cell, he gave a smug walk like he owned the place. George's heartbeat speed up, and his pupils dilated as he walked into the cell. Needless to say, the sight of this man frightened him.

"Yo… Bro…" The Latino asked looking up at George. "What were you talking to yourself about out there, man?"

"Nothing," was the quick reply.

"Let me give you just a little advice bro." The large Latino stepped closer to the bunk. "You got to make some friends in this place to survive. Right now you are not getting off to a good start. See my homeboys, and I want to know what you did to land yourself in here in the first place. You going to tell me nothing to that one too?"

"A quadruple homicide." George looked up from his knees to see if this struck some fear in the large man.

His quick reply was to laugh uncontrollably and look back at his comrades in amazement. "Bro you look like some white collar criminal nothing like homicide. You are gonna have to come up with some better shit than that."

"I'm telling the truth. It's all a big misunderstanding. I go to court later, and my Psychologist will straighten it all out for the judge. I'm sure after that they will let me go." George began to look back down at his knees and grip his legs tighter.

Again the response from the three was laughter. This obviously shook George. He was not sure what the three wanted from him.

George yelled while the three were laughing. "GET OUT AND LEAVE ME BE!"

The three all in unison stopped laughing and the larger one, stepped closer to George, leaving his comrades just outside the threshold of the cell. "Now you listen to me you little faggot," Extending his index finger to point at George.

George extended his index finger at the inmate and yelled, "LEAVE!"

The man was flung out of the cell without any contact being exchanged between the two. He hit his two comrades knocking them all to the ground. The one large man began to yell in agony. As the other two got their bearings, they noticed the huge bruising flesh on his left pectoral.

The thinner man looked up into the cell from his knees. "What the hell did you do to him *Joto!*"

"I will do even worse if you don't all leave me alone." George by this time realized that he was doing this. And that he could control it. "LEAVE!"

The other two men helped the larger one up, but the yelling was attracting a lot of attention. It sounded as if a riot was forming. Men started coming out of their cells to see what the commotion was about. George was able to hear footsteps of people running up the metal stairs. Shouting began, and George had had enough. He looked up and waved his hand at the open door. The metal sliding door operated from the guard station only slammed shut with a loud clank. This, of course, set

off an alarm.

A loudspeaker come on in the block saying

they were on lockdown everyone back to their

cells. One man was left outside George's cell with a

deck of cards in his hands just wondering what to

do.

Chapter 15

Court

Christopher McDonald

After lockdown ended, and the wounded Latino was taken to the infirmary, George was forced out of his cell. The officer led him down the hall making sure to walk behind him. He instructed George to sit on a bench with other inmates. Two other officers with large rifles stood guard while; his hands and feet shackled him to a line of other inmates.

Once the room was filled with inmates a guard pointed at one of the rows of inmates and ordered them to stand. Once up he led them out of the room. Some of the Inmates began to whisper to one another. The officer that was left in the room quickly told them to 'shut it.'

It was time for the other side, the side with George, to head out. Outside George was almost blinded by the bright sun. He saw before him a long

The Interview

white bus like the one that would take you to school as a child. He had never ridden in one but always wanted to. This wasn't exactly what he had in mind when he was wishing.

One single-file line was led to the bus. He noticed once aboard that the bus was situated much like the room he had just left. Each side off the bus only had one long bench running the entire length. Georges Line, of course, was instructed to sit opposite the other. After everyone was down the officers used cuffs to chain the line of men to the legs of the bench. The only way to get up would be to rip the entire thing off the floor.

The ride was uneventful to the courthouse, because like before, no one could talk. One officer drove while the two with guns walked the isle between the prisoners.

Once at the courthouse the bus pulled up to a garage door that had a keypad. The officer driving punched in the code. Once inside George noticed they were going down a ramp that took them into the basement.

After the bus was unloaded, the group of men was gathered before a large metal door. The officer in front of the door began to speak. "Here are the rules. Number one you are to remain silent and orderly at all times in the building. If we are walking to or from a hearing and a judge walks by you will all be instructed to face the wall and not look at the person as they walk by. In the holding cell, you will have the same rules as you would back at county lockup. In the courtrooms, hearing rooms, or any other room where there is a judge I suggest you all act like your mother taught you some manners." He nodded to the other guys with guns and pressed a button next to the big metal door.

The large door opened revealing a freight elevator that everyone was ushered into at the same time. All 25 fit. The door closed, and no one pressed a button. The elevator moved all on its own. There was someone else operating it remotely because there were no buttons at all on the inside of the elevator.

Once they had reached our floor they were all ushered off and led down a long hall with offices and conference rooms on one side or the other. Then there was the large Plexiglas room where they were to be housed. The courthouse guard opened the door, and everyone filtered in. Once inside everyone was unshackled one by one and allowed to move around the room. There was one open toilet as usual for all to use.

George watched in amazement at how quickly the room began to form cliques. He wasn't sure if this was the time to be making friends with these guys. Instead, he watched out the door as the guards exchanged conversation and signed off on all the transfer papers.

George watched one by one as people in suits walked past the holding cell not even looking in the room at the people. As if any of them thought they were people at all. Everyone in the building, to George, already presumed them guilty.

George finally took a seat next to the door hoping that this would be over with quickly, and he could go home. He began to think about his case. How would he be able to prove that he didn't do any of this? At least he didn't do it on purpose anyway.

He thought, 'If the judge listens to Dr. Williams he will be able to see that I am innocent. How could he not? I may have had something to do with all of this, but there is no way to prove it. I can't control whatever it is that is happening to me. If I can control it, I'm not sure even how to begin.'

George's attention was dropped for some reason at two men sitting on the opposite side of the room talking to one another about their case. One said to another, "I need you to tell them you had no idea what was going to happen, and you didn't see anything." The skinhead, the man, was talking to, just nodded in agreement.

He continued to focus back on his own thoughts for a moment. 'I may need to try and figure out how this all works. What if we tell the judge this strange story of mind control and he asks us to prove it. I don't know how it turns on and off I can't even tell if Dr. Williams even realizes that is what it is. She is a doctor and will not be able to prove it to him I'm sure." George wasn't even sure if Dr. Williams was on his side.

George had seen the tape though. "The tape will prove it." This thought came out aloud this time, and everyone stopped to look at the strange man in the corner talking to himself.

"Sorry. I was just thinking out loud." George smiled to the men.

The skinhead just said, "Man... Whatever crazy."

The Interview

George went back playing out in his own mind what would happen when he actually got to tell his side of things.

After what seemed like hours an officer entered the room to call a name. His mind raced. 'What if Dr. Williams forgot about him? What if his only chance relied on himself.'

The hopeless feeling resonated from his toes to his head. What if he can't find a way to prove that it was something he couldn't control?

George went back in forth in his mind painting a picture of what he thought this thing was. He has read several books in his life about people with unnatural powers. 'What if this makes me some kind of super hero? What if I can figure out how to control it?'

He thought back on his childhood and reading a story about an extraordinary child named Matilda. She was able to, with some practice, use her powers under her own control. 'What if this is what I have? What if I could learn to control it like Matilda did?'

George had made up his mind. He was going to experiment. He had the perfect opportunity now. He was sitting in a room with a bunch of people. It seemed, unlike Matilda that he only had control over people.

George eyed the room. Wondering how he should start. 'Somehow I pushed that man in jail,' George thought. 'How was I able to do it? I was scared and angry at the same time. This could be what is triggering the whole thing. My emotions?'

The Interview

'Come-on George. You have to be able to do this. I can do this.' George panned the room to find a man standing in the corner propped against the wall looking out the window. 'I wonder if I can nudge him a little?'

George concentrated. He concentrated so hard he could feel the blood rushing through his veins in his forehead. He could feel something, but nothing was happening.

George lifted his hand pointing at the man he was trying to nudge; concentrating even harder. This obviously got him some very strange looks. Not everyone noticed, but the man sitting close to him whispered, "Dude you ok?"

George put his hand down and decided this wasn't working. He turned and looked at the man whispering in his direction and replied, "Fine thanks."

Lucky for George the man in the corner didn't see him. 'How do I trigger this?' He thought. 'Maybe it's the wrong type of person?' He looked and decided to focus on the person who asked if he was ok.

George this time closed his eyes. He imagined what it was he wanted the man to do. He wanted him to slap his leg. He imagined the image in his mind of a man lifting his arm and slamming it down on his leg. He waited for the noise of the slap, but nothing happened. He opened his eyes and looked over. The man was engaged in a conversation with another inmate.

'I'm not doing something right. There has to be a way to trigger this.' George thoughts exploded

The Interview

as he recalled every instance where something strange happened to the people around him.

He recalled the instance with Whitney. He was upset trying to have a civil conversation with her. It wasn't working. He reached for her as he noticed the bus. She just stopped.

He recalled being in the elevator back in the building. 'Why did Whitney stop dead and the people in the elevator do the same?' He thought to himself while staring at his pants. 'I was sad and angry. I was upset. At the time, nothing made any sense to me. I had to push the people out of my way to get onto my floor.'

In the Courtroom, Angelica sat patiently waiting to see the attorney enter. He did after a short while and sat next to her.

"What did we find out? Mr. Carr asked Dr. Williams.

"He didn't do it. I don't know how we can play this, but he did have indirect involvement in the case." Angelica patted at her briefcase nervously.

"What do you mean Indirect? He asked.

"Well, I'm not even sure you would understand. I have been up all night researching paranormal reasons as to how this could have happened. She again patted her briefcase.

He leaned his head down trying to keep his voice low while looking over his glasses. "Dr. Williams, the court, will not accept paranormal activity as the cause of death in these four murders."

The Interview

"Then what the hell do we do? He didn't push his friend on the tracks. The video overwhelmingly shows that. We have no other choice but to try." She said in a low but desperate voice.

"Angelica look." He took off his glasses and rubbed his eyes. "We have one thing to do today and that's to decide how to continue. I have to give the judge your opinion of whether or not he can stand trial. Then we have to enter a plea on each murder. If the video clearly shows that he didn't push his friend then, he will be fine on this charge."

Angelica interrupted before he could start another sentence. The video not only shows George not pushing him, it shows him being flung onto the tracks like a rag doll."

Mr. Carr squinted his eyes trying to imagine what she was describing. "If that's true the Judge is going to want some sort of explanation. Are we sure the video hasn't been tampered with?"

"The police had it in their custody and requested it the proper way. Isn't that the prosecutions problem whether or not it's real?"

"ALL RISE!...." The bailiff yelled at the room.

George sat trying and trying to make someone move under his control. Nothing was working nothing was happening. 'It must be pain related.' He thought.

He pinched his side while closing his eyes. This time he imagined the man at the window punching the window. He again waited for the sound that was to come from the man slapping his leg. Nothing....

Clank... The door opened. A court officer stepped in. "Victor Perez" He announced. The man with the shaved head stood up and started walking towards the officer.

As Victor passed George, he lunged forward at him in a threatening manner causing George to jump. "What are you looking at..." He said

As George jumped the man in the corner next to the window punched the glass with a thud and the man sitting next to George slapped his hand against his leg.

"Everyone, please be seated," The judge said. I understand this will be a long day, and I will try to get to everyone as quickly as possible."

Angelica leaned over to whisper to Mr. Carr. "Is there any way of knowing when we will be up?"

"No, they won't even do a roll call. Everyone was checked in earlier in the back. The judge will pick the case he wants to hear in the order he wishes to hear them."

"Bailiff, I call Victor Perez to stand before the court." The judge ordered.

"Mr. Carr, I told George we would meet with him before the hearing. Where can we do this?" Angelica asked while a tattooed Latino was escorted in front of the judge.

Mr. Carr replied with wide eyes. "This judge does not allow that. Just watch," He pointed to the Latino

The Judge spoke loudly, "Victor Perez... You are accused of three counts of armed robbery. This

The Interview

is a very serious offence. Do you have representation?" He stared blankly at him.

Victor spoke up. "Yeah, I do. He's out there," Pointing to the crowd.

"Will Mr. Perez's attorney pleas approach the bench?" The judge commanded.

A tall, thin man walked from behind Dr. Williams and Mr. Carr to approach the court. "I am Mr. Perez's' attorney," the man quivered.

As the proceedings continued Angelica leaned in to whisper more to Mr. Carr. "He will be furious. Just being brought out here in front of everyone like that."

"That's how this judge works, Dr. Williams." He said looking over his round glasses. I will ask if he will allow bail and if not we can have him transferred to a low-max facility so that we can see him regularly before the trial.

The thought of George staying in jail any longer made her stomach turn. "I hope he gets bail."

George felt some sense of satisfaction from seeing the man strike the glass and his neighbor slapping his leg. He looked at them both in amazement as they looked perplexed as to what just happened.

George leaned over and asked the guy next to him. "Why did you slap your leg?"

"I don't know man. Mind your own business." He replied.

George knew he had the key to this whole thing. He knew he had to practice so he could prove what was happening around him.

The Interview

Then the thought came over him. What if he does prove it? Will they let him off? No... They will just say I knew how to control it all along.

He closed his eyes and imagined the man hitting the glass again while thinking of the cemetery back home, and how it scared him. The sound of the thud against the glass made George smile.

After several hours in the court room the judge called George's case. Dr. Williams began to stand as Mr. Carr tugged on her blouse to remain seated until called. "This judge has authority issues," She said

"Most of them do," he replied.

After what seemed like hours had passed, George was escorted into the court and placed in front of the Judge. "Where is...." That's all he could get out before the Judge snapped back.

"Silence until spoken to!" He commanded

George took a big gulp of air in and said nothing.

"You are accused of a quadruple homicide. One in the first degree, and the other three in the second degree. I see here that I have appointed both counsel and evaluation for you. Have you met with them?"

"Yes sir," was the quick and fearful reply.

The Judge looks up at the overcrowded courtroom. "Are Dr. Williams and Mr. Carr present today? If so please approach."

Dr. Williams and Mr. Carr stood to walk to the front of the court.

The Interview

George, seeing both of them walk to the front, put his nerves at ease a little.

They took their place beside him while the judge read the facts of the case. Learning from past mistakes they all remained silent.

"Dr. Williams, I see here that it was recommended by the police chief to appoint someone to evaluate the defendant due to strange behavior. What I need from you today is to know if George is mentally stable enough to stand trial?" The judge putdown the paper and stared at Dr. Williams.

"You honor. I do believe that he is fully capable of standing trial, But..." She was interrupted.

"Dr. Williams, there are no but's to this matter. Either he can stand trial or he cannot. What say you?" He frowned while speaking to her.

"He is capable," She said after a pause.

"Good," The judge smoothed his demeanor.

George looked at her with a perplexed look on his face. He thought, 'what happened to her telling him I didn't do it? He won't even let her speak for me.'

"Mr. Carr, I see that I have also appointed you to take this case seeing as the defendant is no longer employed and considered low income," the judge looking back at the papers in his hand.

"Have you given the whole rundown to your client? Have you presented the offer from the district attorney?" The judge asked.

The Interview

"Yes sir, I have, and he declined the plea bargain." Mr. Carr spoke quickly.

"I see," said the judge. "Then how will you be entering the plea today?"

Mr. Carr spoke, "not guilty."

The judge looked at George. "Have you agreed to plea not guilty son?"

George said, "yes, your honor."

The judge looked to the other side of the courtroom and said. "Is the state ready to proceed?"

The attorney for the state said with a big grin on his face, "Yes Sir."

"Well then I set the trial to begin one month from today. The defendant is to be remanded to county custody without bail until the trial." The judge slammed the gavel.

"Your honor, if I may," Mr. Carr spoke up after the sound of the gavel.

"What is it Mr. Carr? Make it fast." He said.

"George poses no real threat here and should be placed somewhere less secure than county giving him some freedoms until trial. Also would you reconsider the option of bail? He poses no real threat..." He couldn't finish his thought.

"Mr. Carr... He poses all the threat in the world. He is accused of killing four people within a matter of an hour. I will not be the judge to set him free on bond no matter how much it is." The judge straightened himself. "If you also think I will put him somewhere that he can bake cupcakes with Martha Stewart you also have another thing coming."

The Interview

Mr. Carr replied, "I understand. Will you at least allow the doctor and I regular access to George until the trial? Also allow us a counsel with him before he returns to county in the courthouse?"

"I have no other choice but to allow this. Bailiff, please escort the three to a conference room." The judge ordered and called the next case.

Once the door shut on the conference room, George said. "What just happened in there? I thought I was going to go home today!"

"George with all fairness you didn't give me much time to brief you on the procedure. You wanted to talk to Dr. Williams." Mr. Carr said sharply.

George cried out as he slammed his cuffed fist on the table. The light in the room dimmed. He looked at the two and said. "What now?"

"George, the prosecutor, is seeking the death penalty. We have no other choice but to fight with everything we have." Mr. Carr replied.

Dr. Williams spoke up as she placed her hand on his shoulder. "With some luck we can beat this George."

George said, "With some luck... All we have is a tape. That gets me off on one charge. What about the other three? There are mixed stories about that, and you know I will hang for this."

"George we are going to do everything we can." Mr. Carr said while looking at his shoes.

George felt the doubt in the two of them. He could hear their thoughts, almost. He knew what this meant for him. He could see it on their faces. He had all but given up hope.

"George once you get settled into county I will be by in the morning to see how you are. You heard the judge; he can't keep us from you." Dr. Williams tried to sound soothing the nerves and desperation was in her voice.

"George I will be by in a couple of days to see how you are as well and fill you in on any progress we have made." Mr. Carr is never taking his eyes off his shoes.

"That's fine Dr. Williams I will see you in the morning. I guess let them take me off to county. I have no other option at this point." George paused. "Maybe I will have figured a way out of this mess by tomorrow."

"That's the spirit," Mr. Carr replied.

"I will see you tomorrow George." Dr. Williams said. The doctor and attorney turned to leave. George said nothing while they walked out.

Chapter 16

What Happened

"Dr. Williams...."

Can you hear me?" a soothing voice said.

"Dr. Williams..."

Dr. Williams began to raise her head from the table. She notices the sound of the voice. She also noticed the sound of the room she was in.

After careful observation, she realized as she raised her head from her arms she was talking to her assistant John. John the one she had handpicked to take under her wing as a doctoral candidate and assistant.

"John... Why did you let me sleep so late?" Dr. Williams asked.

John replied, "I woke you as instructed."

"I need Starbucks white mocha."

"It's on its way Dr. Williams." She looked at the mirror she was as familiar with as an interrogator.

The Interview

"What happened Dr. Williams?" John asked.

"John what the fuck do you mean?" Looking around the room, she realized that she was in a situation that was all too familiar. Her head ached, and her muscles were sore.

"Why did you do it Do Williams?" John asked.

Dr. Williams raised her hands to speak in a dramatic way and noticed that they were chained. She looked long and hard at her hands.

"John... What is this?" She said.

"You don't know?"

"NO... What is this" She said franticly.

"They thought it would be much easier for me to talk to you given the circumstances." John said.

"What the fuck circumstances do you mean?" She looked down at her wrists were in chains.

"John why am I in cuffs?" She demanded.

John paused and took a minute. "You don't remember?" he asked.

"If I remembered why would I be freaking out now?" as she turned she noticed she was in an interrogation room much like the one she listened to George. She noticed the one-sided mirror where she watched the video about the subway.

"Where is George?" She asked.

"You don't know?" he asked looking at the mirror.

"Of course I don't fucking know. "She said. "Last I remember Mr. Carr and I were in the courthouse conference room talking to George."

At this point, she realized she was being interrogated. "Wait... What am I doing back in the precinct? Today is the day I go see George..."

"You don't know?" John asked.

The Interview

"John Fuck You. I know who is on trial here..." She said

"Don't you?"

With that question, she realized it was she on trial. She realized that she was in the interrogation room. She was the one subject to the questioning. 'But why?' She thought.

"John you better start giving me some fucking answers." She slammed her fist on the table. The lights in the room dimmed, and she could see people's shapes on the other side of the mirror.

John said, "Dr. Williams I don't know if you are playing me now or what? I am just going to shoot you straight."

"That's all I ask John."

"I need you to try hard. What is the last thing you remember? He asked.

"I told you I was in the conference room with George and Mr. Carr," was the reply.

"That was yesterday." She looked at him like he was crazy.

"What did you mean yesterday?" She shrilled.

"So you are telling me you have no memory of today at all? Either you are playing one big game here, given your training or you really don't know." John sat back in the interrogation chair.

"John just tell me what the fuck is going on here." She demanded. "Before I go crazy."

"Well, Dr. Williams, you went to go see George at county today. You checked in and waited for about an hour for him to be transferred to an interview room. The conversation was not recorded by you this time and, of course, was not recorded by the jail. All we have is the video

323

The Interview

footage and one witness, the guard outside the room."

"Witness to what?" She demanded.

"Let me get there." He said abruptly. "After you went in you and George talked a bit. You then got up and went to the door and knocked. The guard posted said you asked him for a pot of coffee and two cups. Does any of this ring a bell?"

"No…" She said with tears of fear in her eyes. "What happened next, John?"

"Well, you and George seemed to be having a good conversation. You embraced his hands. The guard arrived with a glass pot and two-Styrofoam cups. You poured for both of you and sat back down.

The guard remembers nothing after this but a huge cry of agony from you."

Her eyes dilated. "Me… What happened?"

He continued, "Well after you and George drank the coffee you two embraced hands again. The room dimmed, and the camera went fuzzy for a second."

She started to tear up thinking, 'What could come next?'

"When the camera came into focus, and the lights were back on their normal hue you had the coffee carafe in your hand." She gulped while listing to the story. "You hit the glass on the corner of the table. It shattered leaving a valuable weapon."

"No… I could not have…" She said.

"Let me finish." He said. "George sat back in his chair and looked at the ceiling." Dr. Williams grimaced as she thought she knew what was next.

The Interview

"You took the broken carafe and slid it across his neckline.

He sat there bleeding, and you took a seat drinking more coffee while he bleeds out."

"John this is not true! This could never happen I would never." She paused.

"What," John said? Did you remember something?"

"George has the power to control people's minds he must have done this." She said franticly

"Dr. Williams you are talking like a crazy woman now. Do you really think this is a defense? George willed me to kill him?" He asked.

"No...!" The lights dimmed in the room as she slammed her fist on the table again.

"See the lights just dimmed. Just like they did when George did it. He must have passed a little of it onto me." She said in a panic.

Dr. Williams you know they have been working on the power grid in the area. It's due to the city upgrading power stations." John said with a sigh.

Dr. Williams knew it wasn't the power grid. She knew what to do…